CHASING DESTINY

**Center Point
Large Print**

**This Large Print Book carries the
Seal of Approval of N.A.V.H.**

CHASING DESTINY

Stephen Overholser

CENTER POINT PUBLISHING
THORNDIKE, MAINE

This Center Point Large Print edition
is published in the year 2009 by arrangement with
Golden West Literary Agency.

The text of this Large Print edition is unabridged.
In other aspects, this book may vary
from the original edition.
Printed in the United States of America.
Set in 16-point Times New Roman type.

ISBN: 978-1-60285-350-8

Library of Congress Cataloging-in-Publication Data

Overholser, Stephen.
  Chasing destiny / Stephen Overholser.
    p. cm.
  ISBN 978-1-60285-350-8 (library binding : alk. paper)
  1. Large type books. I. Title.

PS3565.V43C47 2009
813'.54--dc22

2008035461

To Linda, with love

Chapter One

"No tragedy is so great that it fails to bring good fortune to some poor fool."

That was the adage spelled out for the edification of my classmates and me. Whenever the day's lesson turned to history, those words were scrawled on the blackboard by Mr. Porter, our teacher in Columbia's one-room schoolhouse. From philandering preachers to phony physicians, he was ever alert for hypocrites to skewer with what he perceived to be his rapier-like wit.

I well remember the soft scraping sound of white chalk clenched in his bony fingers, the rounded end pressed to black slate as he formed each letter. I well remember, too, Mr. Porter's hunched shoulders and bowed neck as he stepped back from his handiwork, squinting through steel-rimmed eyeglasses, lips moving. Over the years such poses had earned him the whispered nickname of "Icky," short for Ichabod.

At 3:15 in the afternoon the lessons would be erased by the student of the week, a poor fool assigned to the after-school tasks of cleaning chalkboards and clapping felt erasers together in muted applause to send clouds of fine white powder drifting skyward. Another poor fool lugged the trash and stove ashes to the pit out back, while a third dry-mopped the oiled plank floor from the

United States map on one wall to the state map of Colorado on the opposite side of the room.

None of us questioned the wisdom of our schoolmaster's pet adage. Out of an enrollment of nineteen students ranging in age from six to unknown, no one was willing to stand and challenge or even question the learned man on an issue of such magnitude. For myself, only later in life would I search for meaning and in time come to disagree with his contention cast by hard-edged cynicism that wisdom lurked in shadows.

The teacher never told his students that a cynic must find fault in others to prove his own virtue, that cynicism represents a loss of hope akin to death of the spirit. No, in those days of squirming in a carved-up, notched, and gouged student desk bolted to the floor, I daydreamed while Ichabod held forth. Eyebrows arched, he spoke forcefully from his position of authority on a raised platform at the front of the schoolroom, and mainly I hoped he would not call on me as his fiery gaze swept past.

I did not know the wages of cynicism then. In truth I did not give much thought to any of it, particularly on that sunny day after school when we heard about the murder of Mr. Roger Simms.

Mr. Simms was a prominent cattleman in the north sector of the county, his Bar-S a two-day ride from Columbia on a good horse. Like most farmers on the fringe of town, my father was merely acquainted with the rancher. In those days there was an unspoken social hierarchy that placed cattlemen on a higher rung than the one occupied by farmers. One might say the rancher's brand was a sort of crest, heraldry without all the fuss and pomp of feudal pageantry.

My father and Mr. Simms had been introduced long ago by the storekeeper, Mr. Knowles, during a Saturday shopping trip to town. Beyond that, Father did not acknowledge the man other than to greet him with a nod and perhaps the slight lift of a hand if he was driving the wagon when the cattleman passed by mounted on a custom saddle on a fine horse.

On the day of the murder a farrier discovered the front door to Simms's ranch house standing open—unusual in stinging horsefly country. In the house he found the floor safe open, too, with papers strewn about. The latch of a lock box had been cut by a hammer and cold chisel from the tack room out in the horse barn, the box itself emptied of cash. Mr. Simms lay sprawled on the floor, shot to death on the day he was to have met the payroll for his Bar-S crew.

Owner, cook, and bank teller rolled into one, Simms was a bachelor, a dawn-to-dark rancher of the old school. With the hands tending critters in far-flung pastures, the killer had free rein of the place for several hours. He had stepped in blood and tracked up the floor as he helped himself to the contents of the pantry and liquor cabinet. Then he stole a saddle horse out of the corral—a fatal error.

That horse awaited the farrier. The killer left a dim trail on dry ground, telltale impressions of unshod hoofs. The tracks were readily picked up four days later by the posse Sheriff Hale had dispatched from Columbia. The tracker, Noah Locke, pointed to irregular strides and reported the stolen mount had pulled up lame.

Bobby Eckstrum was run to ground, slain by one hell of a long shot from a Sharps .50 in the hands of Noah Locke. That round from an old buffalo gun was said to have reached 1,000 yards. True or not, the feat entered local folklore, to be told and retold in saloons and livery barns throughout the county, and even the state. Locke, variously portrayed over the years by our resident scribe as "Colorado's colorful character in Columbia," and "the last of the genuine frontiersman ranging from peak to plain," was now described in newspaper accounts as a "steely-eyed marksman," and "a skilled gun hand from the pioneer era."

According to posse men, Locke had cocked the Sharps and stood in the stirrups the moment their quarry was sighted. He snugged the butt plate to his shoulder, drew aim, and squeezed the trigger.

The report was deafening. In the blink of an eye, the impact of the .50-caliber bullet spilled the fleeing man out of the saddle, "dead before he hit the ground," as folks liked to say.

Perhaps so. There was no denying the fact that the heavy bullet packed a punch. It was designed to stop a charging bull buffalo, and the force of this slug blew open the killer's head like an overripe cantaloupe thrown to the ground.

Locke was no braggart, but he was not one to decline free beer at the bar of the Sunflower Palace in recognition of his feat, either.

"Danged lucky shot," he allowed, wiping beer foam from a chalk-white mustache drooping down to fleshy jowls. "Danged lucky."

Such professed modesty only added to his credibility in our parts. As to Bobby Eckstrum, if drunkenness, urinating in public, and vagrancy counted, the crime was not the first he had committed in Columbia. But it was by far the most heinous.

"That bastard killed a good man."

"Got what he deserved from Mister Sharps."

"Old Noah saved us the trouble of knottin' a noose."

"Damn' sure did."

Folks wondered where the payroll had gone. It was no secret Roger Simms paid his ranch hands in cash at the end of the month. He held the money in his floor safe for the convenience of Bar-S cowhands, most of them with deposit and withdrawal transactions meticulously entered in his ledger book.

Ranch hands were questioned by Sheriff Hale, and all of them were cleared. A search for the money was undertaken. No cash was in the ranch house, the horse barn, cow shed, or other outbuildings. Even the toilet pit was probed with a long-handled irrigator's shovel. A total of $4.70 was found in the pockets of the dead man—along with two quart bottles of bourbon in stolen saddlebags. The only other physical evidence was a set of bloody boot prints on the floor. Smeared as they were, anyone could see the toes were blunt—not the pointed toes of boots meant for the stirrup.

Bobby might have hidden the payroll and the saving accounts so carefully noted in Simms's ledger. Or, as some folks speculated, an accomplice might have been involved. Everybody was talking about it. For me, the mystery deepened the morning I came upon my classmate, Destiny Eckstrum. I found her sobbing in her grief.

A couple of weeks had passed since the corpse had been brought in by the posse, and Destiny had not attended school since then. We had all heard about the shot fired by Mr. Noah Locke, as well as the condition of the body. Slung across the back of a burro the posse men had found running loose, the remains of Bobby Eckstrum had been interred without comment in the cemetery north of town. Then came that morning on my way to school when I heard someone crying down by Antelope Creek.

I stopped and listened, at first thinking an animal was there, injured. Leaving my books and lunch box beside the road, I made my way through a stand of cottonwoods downslope to the bank of the creek. There, hunched down in tall grass by slow-moving water, Destiny sat with her hands pressed to her face.

I pushed my eyeglasses up on the bridge of my nose. I saw scuffed, oversize shoes blackened with stove soot instead of the Black Jack Polish everyone else used. Around her neck was an orange and maroon scarf, carefully knotted, and she wore the faded red-checked gingham dress that she always wore in warm weather. Knees drawn to her chest now, she slowly rocked back and forth while I edged closer.

Aware of me, she pulled her hands away from her face. I saw puffy eyes and cheeks reddened from tears when she looked up at me. Neither of us spoke. Her schoolbooks lay in the grass nearby. No lunch box, as usual. Mr. Porter might well have characterized this encounter as a tableau, an elegiac pose fraught with meaning and worthy of a quatrain or two—but, to my mind, the situation was plain enough. Destiny Eckstrum had started for school this morning, but her tears would not stop. She got this far, and folded.

I had overheard whispers of her parentage among grown-ups. Mother unknown, Bobby Eckstrum was believed to be Destiny's father. He had been raising her, if you could call it that, for the last year and a half since their arrival in Columbia from who knew where.

A jack-of-all trades, master of none, Bobby was one of those handy men who took a stab at any task offered to him. He worked at chores in town and on surrounding farms like ours. Half sober, he was a middling worker who did not object to taking his noon meal on the back stoop of his employer for the day. He often took home a pail of milk and a hard-boiled egg or two for Destiny. Bobby could be industrious, certainly a laborer with enough skill and energy to make folks wonder why he did not simply work, eat, sleep like the rest of us.

I suppose we all knew the answer. Bobby Eckstrum was a drunk. His "driving force in life," as Mr. Porter might have phrased it, was to slug down the next drink. The longer his estrangement from Mr. Barleycorn, the deeper his scowl, the shorter his temper. Some folks feared him, others flat out distrusted him, and most wished he would leave Columbia for good. Even so, he kept a roof over Destiny's head, and let her grow like a weed, as they say.

Some folks tried to help them. Food baskets were left by the door of their shack. Footgear and articles of clothing were donated, including the frayed, gaudy scarf Destiny wore constantly. Father and daughter received visits from Bible thumpers intent on raising hell and preaching the devil out of Bobby Eckstrum's poor soul. To no avail. He still downed a pint of coffin varnish before staggering out of his tar-paper shack in search of the day's wages.

Upon earning some cash for performing such tasks as splitting wood for Mrs. Hawkins, replacing pickets in the Widow Bartlett's fence, mucking out stalls down at the Columbia livery, or clearing ditches of weeds and wind-blown trash for Sheriff Hale, he lurched to the nearest deadfall. There, bleary-eyed and tremulous, he left Sobriety behind and drank himself to Oblivion. Such was his routine, whether townspeople approved or not.

Destiny was as scrawny as an alley cat. Folks worried about her. Ladies in town invited her to live in Denver in the Sarah Harmon Home For Girls. 190 miles away from Columbia, it was an orphanage promising to feed, clothe, and house "older girls in unfortunate circumstances."

Nothing doing. Destiny promised to run if anyone tried to put her in that place or any like it.

Through it all, from the heat of summer to wintry cold, she had maintained a loyalty to her father that brought grudging respect from those who knew. In truth, she tried to make do with what they had. Which wasn't much.

Now Bobby Eckstrum was dead, brained by a bullet from a .50-caliber Sharps in the hands of an old-timer. Destiny stayed alone in the Eckstrum shack, I heard, until the Widow Bartlett came and got her. She took her in while folks figured out what to do.

"My pa din't kill Mister Simms."

That's what Destiny said to me the morning I

found her huddled in the tall grass growing along Antelope Creek. I remember her blonde hair was combed and held in place with a tortoiseshell pin. Her dress was pressed, clean except for a green smear on her hip from dew-dampened grass. She was thin, but not gaunt, simply a long-limbed, rangy girl who had not yet filled out to womanhood.

That notion passed through my mind as I tried to figure out what to say or do. In her own way Destiny was a formidable presence, a twelve-year-old girl older than her years by a century. Her blue-eyed gaze projected a certain energy and determination one felt without being able to capture in words.

We were in the same class. Even though I sat one row away and two seats down from her, I did not know her, not well. Like most boys, I cast darting glances her way in the schoolroom, mystified by the female psyche. In Greek mythology, according to readings from Ichabod, the goddess Psyche was the personification of the soul. Beyond answers written on a test, I did not give that premise a whole lot of thought, either.

During recitation I watched her more closely while she stood at the front of the room, head bowed under the gaze of Mr. Porter. Her voice was low and tentative as she recited passages from Gray's "Elegy Written in a Church Courtyard," and memorized verses from Keats's "Ode on A Grecian

Urn." Neck craned as though he had gone deaf, Ichabod invariably commanded her: "Speak up, Miss Eckstrum! Speak Up!"

At recess I was too shy to talk to her, or to any girl, in part fearful of the ribbing I would take if I succeeded in capturing her attention even for a moment. The other part was not knowing how or where to start. It was safer to play ball, roll barrel hoops with a stick, or engage in games of swift pursuit, chases that sometimes put girls and boys on the same trajectory. On occasion, in the undulating surfaces of that playground in a sea of grass, I found myself chasing Destiny.

"Pa din't rob anybody, either."

Destiny raised her gaze to meet my eyes, as though daring me to express any doubt at all. In the distance the school bell pealed. Father would tan me if I was late.

"My pa din't even own a gun," she went on. "He used to, but he swapped it for a quart. Trigger or something was broken, anyway. That's what he told me."

Torn, I stood there on the grassy bank of the creek and stared at her.

"Tell the sheriff," I mumbled at last.

"Sheriff Hale din't believe me."

In an outburst then, Destiny repeated all that she had said to the lawman. Her father had been too "sick" to do much of anything; he was afoot with no means of reaching Simms's ranch house from town; he was physically incapable of committing any crime other than fouling his trousers while "sleeping."

Sheriff Hale had posed the defining question: "If that ain't your pa in the pine box we burr-ied, then who in hell is it?"

Destiny cried. Her voice choked in the retelling, her words lost in sobs wracking bony shoulders. Hearing no credible answer to his question, Sheriff Hale declared the case closed.

Closed, I suppose, until that morning when I asked Destiny if she knew who had robbed and murdered Mr. Simms. Her answer came in a halting voice.

"Sheriff Hale . . . din't listen to me. . . ."

"I'll listen," I said.

The school bell rang again. I knew I would be marked tardy, and take a tanning at home for sure.

Our eyes met and held. Destiny looked at me in a way no girl had ever looked at me before. Another long moment passed between us before she broke the silence.

"Uncle Loy . . . Pa's brother . . . brought a bottle . . . Pa and him . . . left town . . . leading a burro."

I did not say so aloud, but I was thinking about that body slung over the back of a long-eared burro, wrists bound to ankles by a strand of wire. Folks said the corpse was hatless with familiar bushy brown hair tousled, the head caked with dark blood and shards of white bone, an eye dangling from its socket. "Plumb mashed in" was the description of the skull offered by posse men, a sight as gruesome as any ever seen in Columbia.

All of that flashed through my mind, and I wondered if what she had just said about her father could be true. I have to admit I did not know if she was telling me the truth, or if she was merely shoving pain away. Maybe she did not want to believe her father had killed and robbed a man, and was himself dead now. When hurt runs deep and the pain is beyond measure, we tell ourselves stories—and we believe them. For a while, anyway.

At the end of the school day I was headed for the door and freedom when Mr. Porter stopped me.

"Mister Michael Jennings."

I halted and turned to face him as the other students filed out.

"A word with you, please."

With Mr. Porter, it was never just a word, and once again he proved it when I crossed the schoolroom and stood before his desk, straw hat in my hands.

"You were tardy this morning."

"Yes, sir."

"First time this year."

Suddenly aware of my eyeglasses, I pushed them up on the bridge of my nose.

"Yes, sir."

"Reason?"

I shook my head.

"Everything in life is cause and effect, Mister Jennings," he said. "You must have a reason."

I knew if I told him, the crime would only deepen for me, and perhaps come back on Destiny. She had not attended school that day. Either way, I figured telling the whole story would do no good—for me, or for her.

"Reason?" Mr. Porter repeated.

I shook my head again.

"All right then, I shall leave it to you."

I knew what that meant. It was up to me to tell Father and take the punishment that came with my confession. If I did not tell him, at some later date Mr. Porter would. By then, of course, the severity of the tanning would be increased tenfold.

On the way home, I was stopped by a whisper. In afternoon shadows cast by cottonwood trees in full leaf I saw a slight figure emerge and raise a hand, beckoning. I put my books and lunch box down, briefly thinking of some ethereal nymph from Greek mythology as described in Classical texts read aloud by Mr. Porter—until I saw her in the trees.

"Destiny," I said. "You've been here all day?"

"Missus Bartlett thinks I went to school," she replied. "But I've been practicing."

"Practicing what?"

"Come here. I'll show you."

I left the road and followed her into the trees. I

discovered my theory about her was all wrong. She had a plan, and she was enacting it. On a patch of ground by the creek she had spread out clothing, scissors, needles, a thimble, and spools of thread.

"Missus Bartlett is teaching me to sew," Destiny said. "She says a girl like me needs a trade. A good seamstress can work anywhere, any time. How else can I expect to survive?"

I nodded agreement, hearing an echo of Mrs. Bartlett's heartfelt advice in Destiny's voice.

She went on: "I'm cutting Pa's clothes down to fit me. It's called alteration. Oh, and, Michael, look." She reached to a pair of boots with run-over heels and soles with holes. "Pa's boots," she said.

I pushed my eyeglasses up on my nose and looked at the footgear. With pointed toes and two-inch tapered heels, the boots were designed for the man who earned his living in the saddle.

"Somebody left them at our door last year," she said. "They fit me pretty good if I put on two pairs of socks."

She glanced in the direction of the schoolhouse. "I hope Missus Bartlett doesn't talk to Mister Porter before I leave. I don't want her to find out I missed school."

"Leave . . . you are . . . leaving?"

"If I stay here, I'll be sent to a home for girls. Michael, I'll never go back. . . ." Her voice trailed off.

"Where are you going?" I asked.

"Revlis," she replied. She added: "Don't tell anyone."

I stared at her. Revlis was a mining town perched high in the Rocky Mountains west of Columbia. I had never been there, but I remembered the odd name—silver spelled backwards. Clever, perhaps, but if such cartographic creativity was intended to bring good luck to a mine district, it failed. In town we heard the whole region had shut down after the Silver Crash of 1893.

"Pa talked about silver mines near Revlis," she said. "After the crash, he went to Owl Cañon with Loy to work in the gold mines." She leaned close to me. "Michael, I don't know who was riding that horse from Mister Simms's corral. I don't know who the posse killed, either. Pa and Loy are brothers. They look a little bit alike." She paused. "I'll find out."

"Find out," I repeated.

"Find out if he's alive." She eyed the boots as she posed a question. "Michael, do you think I can pass for a boy? Men will leave a boy alone, won't they?"

A look of uncertainty crossed her face. I figured this was the first time she had stated her plan aloud, and the entire notion seemed foreign to her—yet at once I sensed her determination to see it through, no matter the cost.

"Won't they?"

I shrugged. I did not know how to tell her, but every aspect of her plan lay well beyond my experience. My inability to express a suitable answer seemed to frustrate her.

"Michael, you're the smartest boy in the whole school," she said. "You'll probably be a professor like Mister Porter someday. I want to know what you think."

I should have been flattered by her opinion of me, but in truth I was self-conscious about the eyeglasses. At age twelve my vision beyond twenty feet was fuzzy. Two other students wore eyeglasses, but only mine were steel-rimmed like Ichabod's. So great was my aversion to being tarred with the "Icky" brush, sometimes I squinted and did not wear them at all.

Hands on her hips in a no-nonsense pose, Destiny cocked her head a few degrees to the left. "That's why I waited for you. Tell me. You have to tell me. If I cut my hair and if I'm wearing Pa's clothes, can I pass for a boy?"

"I guess so," I said. I added: "Revlis is a long way from here. It's in the mountains somewhere. . . ."

"I know, I know," she broke in. "I'll follow Antelope Creek upstream. I looked at the map in school. As long as I follow the creek to the mountains, I'll come to those mine camps sooner or later."

She added with a smile: "Don't worry about me."

Bent over at the waist, my trousers were bunched around my ankles when father took his belt to me.

In one stinging lash after another, he issued my punishment. He believed I was guilty of the crime of dawdling on my way to school. I had not told him otherwise.

"Next time you'll get a *move* on . . . get there at first bell . . . won't you?"

I did not reply. I kept my back to him, a gesture that stirred his ire. He lashed me again with the belt and raised his voice to demand compliance. With my jaw clenched tightly enough to bust teeth, I uttered no sound. Even at its worst, when pain radiated down the backs of my legs like fire, I thought about Destiny.

I had kept our encounter to myself. Now, as I withstood Father's lashings, I was determined never to give in, never to yield to pain.

"Won't you?"

I stole a glance at him. Broad-shouldered and bull-necked, Father was not a man to cross. He was a skilled farmer, strong and capable of handling any chore or manhandling any critter on the place. When it came to handling his family, he was lost.

Mother had left Colorado two years and three months ago. Taking my two sisters, Marie and Eva May, with her, she packed their belongings in two trunks. Escorted by Sheriff Hale on horseback, they left the farm in a coach driven by two men from town. By way of Denver, she returned to Chicago where "her people" resided.

I stayed behind and helped Father. Not that he

needed me. Perhaps he required my help to keep up with chores, but if some other reason bolstered that parental decision, I was not informed of it. I merely did what I was told.

I well remember Mother's tears and her long embrace when she departed. Even Marie and Eva May hugged me that day. I did not know what to make of it at the time, but none of them embraced Father or even spoke to him. Heads bowed, eyes averted, they left in the coach. Not until later did the full weight of a larger truth bear down on me.

The dawning moment had come when I accompanied Father to Mr. Knowles's general mercantile on a Saturday shopping trip. I overheard a hiss of whispers from a cluster of women in the store. Something about the intensity of their hushed voices stilled me. They did not know I stood behind them, one aisle away at the hard candy bins.

"She left him."

Those were the words I overheard. Mrs. Knowles and the other ladies shared tight-lipped nods and cast surreptitious glances at my father. He stood at the counter while his bill was tallied. A moment later the women spotted me. They dispersed with a sudden rustle of starched fabric like doves taking flight. Until that moment I had believed Mother and my sisters had merely gone away. At some point they would return. After all, if the separation was permanent, wouldn't Mother have said so?

She left him.

Those words whispered with such force and finality were revelatory. For the first time I realized I might never see my mother and sisters again, at least not until I was old enough to travel on my own. Father was not a man to leave the farm or travel farther away than Columbia under any circumstances, and now Mother was ensconced in Chicago with relatives.

Father had tanned me before, but this time he must have been enraged by my stoicism. He drew back the belt as far as he could reach. When he laid it on me, I screamed.

Breathing hard, he hit me again, and backed away. I sobbed like a child while he slapped the belt against his open hand in one final gesture of authority. Refusing to look at him was my sole avenue of defiance, and I used it until he turned and stomped out of the room.

I eased my trousers up and faced the doorway where Father had gone. I stood there a good long while.

Destiny was absent from school the next day, too. Thoroughly distracted from morning to afternoon by my pain and by the sight of her empty school desk, I kept wondering if she had left Columbia.

Curiosity got the better of me. The moment school was dismissed, I gritted my teeth and ran— or hobbled—all the way to the shack on the edge of town where she had lived with her father. I figured she might be there now, rather than at Mrs. Bartlett's house.

I was right. When I approached the shack, the door fashioned from scraps of lumber and odd pieces of tar paper eased open.

Surprised to see me, Destiny blinked rapidly as she stepped through the aperture into the glare of mid-afternoon sunlight. I stared at her head. Corn-silk hair was cropped as short as a boy's.

Destiny ran her hands down her front and over her hips, smoothing faded gingham fabric while ducking her head in a self-conscious gesture. She wore her father's boots, a threadbare dress, and that orange and maroon scarf. My jaw locked up as we faced one another.

I had been thinking about what she had said yesterday, all of it. The enormity of the trek she proposed came to me in bits and pieces. I tried to think it through, and wondered if she had fully grasped it. Had she planned out every detail? Or would she merely strike out on her own, perhaps wandering to her death on the vast prairie?

We looked at one another. She had left the door standing open, and now she glanced over her shoulder. I followed her gaze. My sense was that she was ashamed of the place, too ashamed to let me see in, much less enter. Not that I wanted to. I stood there and struggled to frame my question. All the while I looked at her in strained silence. At last she spoke.

"What are you doing, Michael, coming here?"

I found my voice, if not my brain, and tried to answer. "I wondered . . . wondered if you were still here . . . if you had left yet . . . if you're still going . . . like you said yesterday."

"I'm going."

"You'll need food," I said. "More than you can carry. Water, too, in case the creek runs dry."

"I know," she said.

"But how . . . how will you . . . ?"

I was unable to find the words to finish my question. With another glance back, she turned and gestured to me. "Come here."

She took me behind the shack. A rickety corral confined a scruffy burro, a gray critter with a tail like a worn-out hearth broom. Ears twitching, the critter's large brown eyes followed our every move.

I looked around. Brush and weeds were heaped nearby. On the ground outside the enclosure lay a pair of leather and wicker panniers. Destiny gestured to them with a wave of her hand.

"I've got dried apples, salted beef, and tins. Canteens, too. Two of them." She paused, fingertips touching her scalp experimentally. "I altered Pa's felt hat. It fits pretty good." She turned to the burro in the corral. "He's tame. I hand-fed him. He follows me like a dog. I've got a lead rope, but I won't need it much. He'll carry those packs and tag after me." She added: "At night, I'll hobble him to keep him from wandering."

I took all this in, aware I had underestimated Destiny. She had formulated a plan, and had seen to the details.

I asked: "When . . . when are you leaving?"

"Tomorrow," she said. "Before dawn. I'll leave without awakening Missus Bartlett. I can find my way in the dark to the creek." She paused. "You din't tell anyone."

I shook my head.

Once again we gazed at one another, and for a long and tortured moment neither of us spoke. At last I stepped back and muttered something about going home to do my chores.

She raised her hand in a parting gesture. "Good bye, Michael."

I jogged back to the farm, arriving late enough to draw a stern look from Father, but not so late for him to demand an accounting of my time and whereabouts. We did not speak.

At supper I kept my head bowed, still feeling pain from yesterday—a reminder of my punishment for dawdling. I was aware Father looked at me a time or two with a dulled expression of bovine placidity, but for the most part I avoided his gaze.

Yesterday something had happened between us, something more than a mere tanning. I knew it, and I will always wonder if Father knew it, too. As far as I was concerned, he had driven a wedge between us—unspoken, immutable—a barrier as solid as stone.

My decision that night marked a momentous event in my life, a watershed, as they say. I wish I could lay claim to righteousness. I wish I could point to a showdown between my father and me, some titanic explosion that launched me into manhood and the world.

The truth, I fear, is prosaic. I merely left in the night.

Chapter Two

Like most farms and ranches of the day, slabs of venison and chunks of beef jerky were hung from a rafter or nailed to an inside wall of our barn. As an emergency supply of protein, the preserved meat was placed high enough to be out of the range of a leaping coyote, a clever 'coon, or a wandering wolf—hungry animals drawn out of the night by the potent scent. Dark as a boot heel and nearly as tough, the meat itself—some of it several years old—resembled weathered roofing shakes more than edible meat.

Working by feel and by dim starlight emanating from the doorway, I pried out nails driven through venison jerky. I dropped each piece into a gunny sack with tins of food, extra clothes, and a blanket. To the hodge-podge, I added matches, fishing hooks, and line.

With the gunny sack slung over my shoulder and a Barlow folding knife in my trouser pocket, I left

the farm well before dawn. Except for food, my only real theft was the filching of Father's two-quart canteen. I did not own one, and even though I meant to follow Destiny's route along Antelope Creek toward the headwaters, I knew it was green-horn foolish not to carry water.

Alone in the dark of night, I walked along the bank of the murmuring creek. Water reflected starlight, flowing like quicksilver through clusters of willows. Too dark to see a burro, much less a set of tracks, I had no way of knowing where Destiny was now. She might be some distance ahead, walking swiftly in her long strides, or she might be somewhere behind me—or asleep in the comfort of Mrs. Bartlett's spare bedroom.

I slowed, wondering if she'd had a change of heart, if I should stop and wait for daybreak, or press on. If Destiny was ahead of me, there was no point in stopping here. But if she was following the course of the creek somewhere behind me, when would she catch up?

Instinct told me to keep moving. After daybreak I would cut her trail sooner or later, I figured—unless she had changed her plan altogether. That thought passed through my mind again. Yesterday she had been filled with purpose, set on enacting her plan. Today, though, faced with the grim reality of a long and lonely journey to a place unknown to her, would her determination flag?

Remembering her remark about the threat of being sent to the Sarah Harmon Home in Denver, I doubted she would change her mind. Not now. Later, perhaps. If her trek to the far mountains became torturous rather than merely footsore and exhausting—if her trek became endless and impossible—then she would lose heart.

In that case what would I do? I tried mentally to list the possibilities. Would I continue heading west? Would I turn back? Where would I work—on a farm, a ranch, a mine, the railroad? With an array of choices before me for the first time in my life, I was unable to focus on any one of them. Even though I was determined not to back-track and admit defeat, I wondered what would happen if I faced my father after several days' absence—or several weeks?

A variety of speculations rolled through my mind until I heard a shrill, ear-piercing sound. In a high-pitched stutter, that animal call captured a tonal range midway between a squeal of agony and a stifled sneeze.

Pulled out of my reveries, I stopped and looked back. A faint glow fired the eastern horizon. I pushed my eyeglasses up higher on the bridge of my nose and tried to peer into night shadows, to penetrate pools of darkness not yet chased away by dawn. Somewhere back there, Destiny's burro brayed again.

• • •

"What are you doing here?"

When she caught up with me, Destiny threw that question at me like a stone. In the next instant she jerked the hat off her head and literally threw it to the ground. She moved a pace closer, jaw jutting in her anger.

"Michael, I said, what are you doing here?"

I stared, silenced by her hostility. I had not known what reaction to expect from her, but flaring anger had not occurred to me. Red-faced now, she easily stared me down. I mumbled something about walking with her.

"No! No!"

I lifted my gaze. We eyed one another while the gray burro watched. Dressed in her father's altered clothes, hair cropped, Destiny had succeeded in concealing her gender. Brown wool trousers with shortened braces, a blue flannel work shirt, and a man's jacket and boots made her resemble a smooth-faced boy wearing hand-me-downs.

Placing her hands on her hips in a girlish gesture now, she drew a deep breath. "Michael, if you came here to tell me to go back, I won't."

"I'm not saying you should," I said.

Her eyes narrowed. "Did you tell anyone?"

"No."

"Then why are you here?"

This time she did not stare me down. I met her

gaze. "I'm going west . . . to find work . . . on a ranch . . . somewhere."

She obviously disbelieved me, and waved her hands as though shooing chickens. "Michael, go away! Leave me alone!"

My own anger mounting, I said: "I'll leave you alone if that's what you want. But I will walk toward those mountains. . . ."

"Well, I won't walk with you!" she shouted.

"Then walk alone," I said. "I don't care."

Looking past her, I saw a thin, brilliant band of light on the eastern horizon. "Look."

"What?" she demanded, glancing eastward in a moment of alarm.

"Sunup," I said.

"Oh, that."

"We're wasting time," I said. "Missus Bartlett might send someone to find you. The sheriff, maybe. . . ."

"She won't send that lawman or anyone else," Destiny broke in. "Nobody cares." She eyed me again. "But your pa might."

I stared at her. In truth I had not thought of that. "No matter what happens," I said, "I'm not going back to the farm."

She must have detected a note of finality in my voice, for that remark silenced her. Inwardly I was still reeling. The dispute that had erupted between us caught me by surprise. I had assumed Destiny would welcome my company, and had not given much more thought to it. Proven wrong now, I realized once again that we hardly knew one another.

I said: "Destiny, you are right."

"About what?"

"Leaving home," I replied.

"What about it?"

"I got that notion from you."

"Thought so."

"Doesn't mean we have to stick together," I said. "I'll head west until I find ranch work, or some other kind of job. I don't know what kind. All I know is I want to live on my own."

She studied me.

I took another look at the brightening sky to the east. "I have to get a move on."

As I heard myself give voice to those words, I recognized one of my father's expressions. He was always urging me to hurry. *Get a MOVE on!* Now I heard those words and his inflection in my voice.

Destiny continued staring at me, hands still planted on her narrow hips, head cocked to one side. The pose was at once girlish and defiant. I could see that she still did not believe my account. Hefting the gunny sack over my shoulder, I turned and strode away. In a glance back I saw her expression soften, her face no longer beet-red.

I headed west, walking along the bank of Antelope Creek. I did not look back for a hundred paces or so. When I ventured another backward glance, I saw Destiny coming. Head bowed, she trudged along with the burro obediently following.

Late in the morning I found a patch of shade beside the creek. I pulled off my boots to air out sweaty feet. Destiny had caught up with me. Even though we had not spoken since the argument had flared between us, she seemed to accept the fact that we were traveling together for now.

She moved to the burro's side and unbuckled a pannier strap. Lifting the leather flap, she peered inside. She reached in. I saw her take out two hard-boiled eggs. She stepped into the shade and knelt beside me, offering one to me.

I took it from her hand. She cast a tentative smile at me, and sat in the grass. With the creek's soft sounds nearby, I was reminded of that morning on my way to school when I had found her in tears.

"Michael," she said now, "I'm sorry . . . sorry I was sharp with you."

I said: "I know you didn't expect to see me."

"It's not that," she said. She paused in thought. "You're the only one who knows. I trusted you, and, when I saw you at dawn, I thought you meant to talk me out of leaving. I thought you would tell on me if I din't go back. That's why I lost my temper."

The farmstead, the town, the prairie—these places defined the landscape of my childhood. If the farm-house was the hub of an imaginary wheel, then it could be said I well knew the terrain from horizon to horizon for ten or fifteen miles in any direction. Every stone outcropping, every swell, every clump of brush, every fox and rattlesnake den, every game trail leading to water—features within the circumference of my childhood explorations were familiar. I was comfortable in those places, comfortable where I had hunted rabbits and caught trout, where I had herded cattle and chased runaway livestock, where I had lain on my back on sun-warmed earth to escape bossy sisters, where I had watched hawks dive and eagles soar. From all points of the compass, the horizon had defined my place in this land. Then I walked away from it, all of it.

To the uninitiated, I suppose, the Colorado prairie must seem uniformly drab. Nearly barren under a vast sky, there is a numbing sameness to this land. The plain is cut by a few creeks and countless dry washes—an expanse marked by clumps of rabbitbrush, sage, and cactus.

To my eye, though, this stretch of prairie along Antelope Creek was distinct from the terrain of my boyhood. Striding westward, I felt a vague, tingling sensation—fear of the unknown. Yet at once I was stirred by a keen sense of exploration as though I had tapped into primeval yearnings. I pushed my eyeglasses up on the bridge of my nose and forged ahead. I felt driven to discover all that lay beyond the next swell in the land, and the rise after that, and beyond as we walked toward the setting sun.

Tired and footsore, we camped in the grass beside the creek. To conserve the friction matches I had brought, we did not build a fire. Destiny had made two discoveries that left her exasperated. For all of her planning and gathering, she had forgotten to bring matches. Then she discovered she had forgotten the blanket she had neatly folded and left on the foot of the bed in Mrs. Bartlett's upstairs bedroom. The blanket was a good one, she confided, one that had been donated to her last winter by "anonymous."

After declining my offer to use my blanket, she thought better of it after dark. The night air was warm and still, and even though she slept in her clothes, a cover offered comfort and a measure of security. When she came to me in darkness and stretched out at my side, I spread the blanket over us. The length of her body pressed against me as we lay on our backs and looked up at the stars.

"You said you'd tell me," she said.

"Tell you what?"

"About leaving your farm," she said. "What happened?"

Offering few details, I gave her a brief account of the tanning my father had laid on me. I did not mention the reason I was tardy was that I had stopped and talked to her that morning on the way to school. I did not want her to think I blamed her.

Not that it mattered. Not then. For as I spoke, Destiny drifted off to sleep.

We broke camp before sunrise. Footsore, Destiny walked as long as she could tolerate the pain. We made some progress, but she slowed, and halted.

Awash in the first light of day, she sat on the ground. Her face screwed into a grimace when she pulled off a boot. Her father's wool socks were stained red where blisters had opened and bled. The burro came closer and sniffed at her as though offering sympathy.

An argument flared between us when I suggested we rest. She pointed out the fact that a minor wound like hers would not heal for days. All we could do now was press on. I watched her rearrange the two socks on that foot and pull on a third. She tugged the boot on. Standing, she took a few tentative steps. I watched as she favored that foot. There was no quit in her, as they say, and, even though pained, I could see that she had lost none of her resolve.

In the afternoon the burro suddenly grew restless. I figured a predator roamed nearby, and our long-eared beast of burden had caught a hostile scent. I wiped the lenses of my eyeglasses on my shirt. Looking around, I saw no sign of wolves or coyotes. Nothing unusual was in sight until we topped a rise. I looked back. A lone rider was on our trail.

Chills crawled up my back. I halted and peered at him. Destiny followed my gaze. I heard a sharp intake of breath when she saw our pursuer. Moments later we recognized the mount—a long-legged, riding mule, black as tar.

"Mister Locke," she whispered.

The burro tried to run. I held him fast while Destiny slipped hobbles on his forelegs. We could have fled, but with no place to hide on the open prairie, Noah Locke would simply overtake us. Glancing at one another, we knew without exchanging a word that we could do nothing but wait.

We offered no pretense of a friendly greeting to Mr. Noah Locke. Neither did he. Silent and grave, he stared at us while he approached on his black mule.

The old-timer wore a fringed buckskin shirt, patched wool trousers, moccasins with beaded leggings, and a hatband of rattlesnake skin. A sheathed Bowie knife was belted on his hip. So was a buckskin possibles sack where he carried flint and valuables.

My gaze went to his saddle. Much scarred and weathered, the stock of the famous Sharps rifle protruded from the scabbard.

In Columbia I had passed by this man on occasion. I knew him merely by sight and by reputation. Donning his frontier get-up, Noah Locke was the colorful old-timer of our town. Amid all the marching and speech-making during 4th of July celebrations, he regaled folks with tales of the "wild waste," an idyllic era when trappers followed waterways, when Indians roamed, when prairie schooners sailed, when stars in the heavens were young, as they say. And, of course, he was the deputized citizen who had killed the man identified as Destiny's father.

She still struggled with the burro. Even with hobbled front legs, rear hoofs lashed out, quick as a rattler. Destiny restrained him, but he still tried to back away, head bobbing as though he was in the presence of an unwelcome relative. Perhaps he was, for the mule grew restive, too.

"What do you danged fool kids think you're doing?"

Neither Destiny nor I answered Mr. Locke's barked question. We saw him grimace when he turned his upper body and grasped the saddle horn. Grunting in pain, he swung a leg over and dismounted. After quieting the mule, he turned and gave Destiny a measured look.

"You the Eckstrum girl?"

"Who wants to know?"

I was surprised when she sassed him. Casting a sidelong glance her way, I saw a determined edge in the profile of her face.

"Folks in Columbia, that's who," Mr. Locke answered. He turned to me. "The farmer, Jennings . . . he's your pa?"

I echoed Destiny's rejoinder. "Who wants to know?"

Mr. Locke was not inclined to take any guff from me. Gnarled fist clenched, he advanced a pace. "Get smart with me, young 'un, and I'll knock it outen

41

you. Knock the smart clean outen you. Hear me?"

I stared at him without answering or even acknowledging his rough-voiced query. For a reason I did not know then, any more than I can explain now, I harbored no fear of Noah Locke. He was armed, he growled like an arthritic grizzly, and he had killed a man. Perhaps it was merely youthful naïveté, but I felt no fear as he scowled and issued his threats.

"Mind me," he said. "Both of you mind me."

Hands planted on her narrow hips, Destiny challenged him. "What are you going to do if we don't, Mister Locke? Shoot us?"

He studied her. "I figure you got nothing but hate for me. All I got to say is I didn't know it was your pa when I pulled the danged trigger."

"How do you know it was him?" she asked.

The question silenced him for a moment. "What're you driving at?"

"Maybe you killed my pa," she replied, "and maybe you din't."

He eyed her. "What're you talking about?"

"I had my say with Sheriff Hale," she answered. "Go talk to him. I've got nothing more to say to you." She added: "Leave us alone."

Mr. Locke glowered, obviously weighing his options. He gestured at the panniers. "Reckon I'll have me a look-see in them packs."

Destiny demanded: "You came all this way to rob us?"

"Not perzactly," he said. "Reckon you could say I came all this way to rob a robber."

"What do you mean?" she asked.

With bushy eyebrows arched, Mr. Locke replied: "The payroll's in them packs, ain't it?"

"Payroll," she repeated.

"Don't play dumb," he said. "Ever'body knows your pa stole that-ere Bar-S payroll. He tried to excape on a saddle horse stoled outen Mister Simms's corral. Didn't he?"

"No, he din't," Destiny replied.

"I know for a fact," Mr. Locke continued, "that he didn't have it on him when the posse men turned his pockets inside out. They done ripped his shirt open. Emptied his boots, too. Way I figure, iffen your pa didn't have it on him then, you've got it now." He added shrewdly: "He passed it to you for safekeeping, didn't he?"

Destiny stared at him.

"Open 'em up," Mr. Locke ordered, and gestured to the panniers again.

"Mister Locke, everything in there belongs to us," she said. "Clothes, food, sewing gear, and such." She glanced at me.

I said: "That's the truth, Mister Locke."

He snorted. "Then you won't mind iffen I have me a little look-see."

The old-timer moved to the burro's side and unbuckled the strap of the right pannier. Lifting the flap, he peered inside. He plunged his hand in.

After rooting around and looking at the contents, he moved to the other side and opened the left pannier. He pawed through it, and pulled out a hard-boiled egg. Pocketing it, he thrust his hand back into the pannier. With a sudden curse, he jerked his hand out.

I saw Mr. Locke stare at a droplet of blood on his finger as though eyeing a snakebite. He cast a pained look at Destiny.

"Told you I had sewing gear," she said.

He swore. "Where in hell did you hide that-ere cash money from the Bar-S?"

"How could I hide it?" she asked. "I've never seen it."

Mr. Locke's chest heaved. "You're lying."

"No, I'm not."

"Then why did you run off?" he demanded.

"That's none of your business," she said.

Mr. Locke eyed her. "You fancy yourself big, don't you? I'm a-telling you, you ain't big. Ain't neither one of you big. You'd danged well better get back home. Both of you. Now, hand over the payroll, and git."

Destiny met his gaze in silence.

"Want I should haul you back to Columbia," Mr. Locke demanded, "hog-tied on the back of that-ere ass? I reckon I'll get a ree-ward for my trouble."

"You'll have to shoot us first!" Destiny exclaimed.

Mr. Locke regarded us. He clearly had not expected a pair of danged fool kids to buck him. In the wordless manner of a stand-off, we stared at one another. Locke was outnumbered, and I think he was evaluating the odds. His shoulders sagged.

The moment passed. I saw him give Destiny the once-over twice, an eyebrow cocked as though he had made a discovery. His mood changed. I was less worried about this man gunning us down in cold blood than I was the leer that crept into his eyes.

"Them baggy clothes you're wearing," Mr. Locke said. "Some kinda man's outfit, ain't it?"

I could see that she sensed his intent, too. She stiffened when he moved a pace closer.

"You're carrying that-ere money on you," Mr. Locke said, his gravelly voice deepening. "It's under your danged clothes. Ain't it, now?"

She shook her head, eyes downcast. "Leave us alone, Mister Locke. Just go away and leave us alone."

"Not before you take them clothes off," he said. "Ever' danged stitch."

She shook her head again, avoiding his gaze.

Locke drew his Bowie knife from the sheath on his belt, and waved it. "Reckon I'll slice them baggy clothes right offen your skinny self."

I took two steps toward him, lifting my hands as though warding him off. "No, you won't."

Knife blade up, Mr. Locke's gaze swung to me. He grinned, showing missing teeth. "You fixing to stop me, young 'un?"

I nodded.

"Just how do you aim to do that?" he asked.

I had no idea. All I knew was I could not let him take a knife to Destiny. As it turned out, a distraction was enough to give us the edge. Destiny moved to her left, momentarily drawing Locke's attention away from me.

I had never fought anyone before, but on school grounds I had joined Will Taylor, Joey Bachman, and George Johns in shoving matches. It was a game of dominance that I often won, eyeglasses and all. I had inherited enough of my father's shoulders and girth to prevail in some of those playground contests.

I lunged at Mr. Locke. Closing the distance, I thrust my arms straight out, elbows extended. The heels of my hands punched into his shoulder, driving him away from Destiny. He staggered under the impact of my unexpected move. Arms flailing, Locke nearly went down. The knife fell from his grasp and landed in the dirt at our feet. Awkward and stiff-legged, the old-timer regained his balance.

Destiny pulled the burro around. She backed the critter close to Mr. Locke. A small hoof lashed out, and the old-timer let out a howl. Kicked in the shin, he hopped to his mule. He grasped the saddle horn for dear life and held on, breathing hard.

"Leave us alone!" Destiny shouted. "Go away, and leave us alone!"

Mr. Locke scowled, but issued no more threats. His jaw slack and his leathery face drawn, the fight had gone out of him. He managed to pick up his Bowie knife and sheath it. Thrusting a foot into the stirrup then, he mounted with a grimace and a groan.

Destiny and I looked at one another, barely able to contain our excitement. Never had I felt so exhilarated. As we watched Mr. Locke ride away, we saw a grown-up in defeat. We had won. Looking at one another, we stifled giddy laughter.

We walked until sundown, and camped. While Destiny tended the burro, I cut a sapling growing on the bank of the creek. After catching a grasshopper in the weeds, I walked a short distance upstream, and found a deep pool shaded by cottonwood trees.

I tied my fishing line on the end of the sapling, and baited the barbed hook with the grasshopper. Still kicking, the insect no sooner hit the water than the surface churned, the grasshopper pulled under. I hauled back, setting the hook in the mouth of a native trout nearly a foot long.

Destiny gathered twigs and dry branches, and by the time I caught three more trout, she had a fire going. I gutted the fish with my pocket knife. We cooked them on a willow spit. Discarding scorched skin, we pulled steaming meat away from fine white bones. We ate with our fingers, blowing on the meat to cool it. The meal was topped off with a tin of peaches, the fruit speared by my knife.

In the fading light of evening, Destiny cocked her head at the mournful calls and sharp yips of coyotes. "Do you think Mister Locke will come back?"

I shook my head.

"Why?"

"He thought he had everything figured out," I said, "but you didn't have the Bar-S payroll."

"What if he still thinks the money's under my clothes?"

"Is it?"

"Michael," she said in reprimand.

"If he comes back," I said recklessly, "we'll run him off."

"He's a filthy man, isn't he?"

I shrugged. I had not noticed filth, but I had been close enough to smell soured sweat and see gaps in his yellowed teeth.

"Michael."

I turned to her, seeing self-consciousness and a look of shyness in her expression. "I have to bathe."

Leaving our camp, we walked to the pooling water where I had caught the trout. I pointed to the slow-moving current.

"It's deep," I said. "Jump in."

She considered that, and gave me a playful shove. "All right. But go away. Don't watch." She added a warning. "Remember Actæon."

I turned and walked away as she undressed. Presently I heard water splashing.

I remembered that lesson from Greek mythology. Actæon broke a promise when he observed Artemis in her bath. As punishment, she turned him into a stag and he was killed by his own dogs. Vivid imagery and a spirited reading style made a scene few students of Mr. Porter would forget.

I sat on ground warm from the sun. I tried to find a comfortable position, but my buttocks were still sore. Riding the burro bareback even for a short time had been torturous. I had walked beside him while Destiny rode him for short periods of time.

Now, through a grove of trees, I glimpsed Destiny as she submerged herself. She bobbed up, blowing, and wiped water from her face with both hands.

I thought about her, recalling her demeanor when she had faced Mr. Locke. Life had toughened her. If bravery is the refusal to yield to a superior force, then she had exhibited great courage. In truth I had merely followed her lead. I had seen her defy the man, and heard her sass him. Emboldened, I obeyed a protective instinct by shoving him aside at an opportune moment. The old-timer was neither agile nor strong enough to handle both of us. All he could do was issue threats—empty threats at that. The taste of victory still excited me, as though I had advanced a step or two closer to manhood.

When I returned to our campsite, I found Destiny

wearing her gingham dress and that scarf. She cast a self-conscious glance at me, and ducked her head, a young woman shorn.

"I don't want to look like some rough boy all the time," she explained. "I want to be a girl sometimes." She touched her head and smiled. "A girl who does not need a comb."

So it was at our camps as we crossed the plain. Most evenings Destiny would abandon her boy outfit for girl garments. Even though we had not encountered anyone since Mr. Locke departed, she felt safer in daylight posing as a boy. We concocted a tale to account for our trek in the event we encountered anyone else.

I would introduce myself as Michael, while Destiny posed as my younger brother Joe. We would claim to have left a farm far from here, and we were heading to the mines to rejoin our father after the tragic death of our mother in a raging barn fire. The dramatic aspect of our tale came from Destiny. It sounded plausible to us, but we did not know what we would find in the mine districts.

We were uncertain of the effects of the Silver Crash of 1893. We no longer heard much about it. I knew the price per ounce of silver had dropped suddenly. Investors had lost fortunes overnight, and men left mine districts in droves, broke. But with Columbia far removed from the mountains and the mines, we were largely unaware of the consequences of an economic disaster.

Unlike Destiny, I did not believe my father or anyone else from town would pursue us runaways. Even so, I watched our back trail, alert for dust clouds or other signs of pursuers. Aside from dust devils occasionally spiraling into the sky, I saw nothing but clusters of pronghorn and lone jack rabbits, speedy creatures bounding away when we drew too close.

By the fourteenth day of our trek we were both footsore and foot blistered. We limped along the bank of Antelope Creek. Soaking our feet in the cool caress of the creek relieved pain for the moment, but we could hardly stop every two or three miles to pull off boots and plunge our feet into the elixir. So we pressed on, "ever westward, ever westward," as the pioneers said, feet hurting, and all.

Out of sheer necessity, we took turns riding the burro. Strong as an ox, that long-eared creature was dependable, forgiving, uncomplaining. I well remember those large, soulful eyes while the burro handled both panniers and one passenger without a misstep. Looking back on our prairie crossing, I know Destiny and I could never have made it to the far mountains without that burro.

If heaven exists, I will be amazed to find myself there. But I will not be surprised to see burros wandering gold-paved avenues amid the white-robed believers. Somewhere up there in the heavenly spheres, those gentle quadrupeds tag along after the saved, all of the good folks aglow in their beatific smiles.

With heaven above our heads and earth at our feet, time slid by. In the open prairie the date was not a mere number to be marked off the calendar day by day, any more than time could be measured by a ticking timepiece with thin steel springs driving cogged wheels. Flowing like mercury, time was fluid, an alchemy as strange as mirrors melting into silvery pools.

In that way we lost track of time altogether. The prairie had sucked it out of us. I no longer knew how long ago we had left home. Was it three weeks? Four? More?

On the western horizon the Rocky Mountains were dark shadows. The storied cañons and mining camps hardly seemed closer now than when we had first sighted them.

Far from the terrain of my childhood, the endless prairie took a toll on both of us. The creek flowed steadily, but the hot sun, the bone-dry air, and the sheer vastness of open prairie had a demoralizing effect. I saw jaw-jutting determination in Destiny's face fade to slack-jawed exhaustion.

I worried about her. In familiar surroundings we had considered ourselves to be grown-ups. We were independent, supremely confident, and we believed no one could stop us. Such was our conviction. But we erred. With no specific knowledge of the distance involved, we failed to pace ourselves. More serious than blisters or sunburns, exhaustion set in. Even the burro staggered. We reached a point where our young bodies needed rest—a great deal of rest.

Halting, we camped for three days. We lounged beside the creek, and reclined in the shade of cottonwoods. We spoke of the inconsequential, of immediate concerns, of school, of anything to avoid confronting terrors. For I think we both harbored one, overriding fear—our destination lay beyond our reach, and we had come too far to turn back. I did not raise the possibility, and neither did Destiny.

In truth, we had no real choice. We had to continue hiking westward, one dizzying, uncertain step after another. On the morning of the fourth day, believing we had recovered our strength, we pressed on. Footsore and legs aching, our enthusiasm was short-lived.

Like a silent storm, fatigue overtook us. Destiny stayed aboard the burro most of the time now, but her grasp was weak, and she was barely able to stay aboard. She leaned against me while holding on. Nights, she wept as she lay at my side under the blanket. I held her, feeling her thin body quiver as though she had taken a chill.

Terrors stabbed me, too, cutting deep, as I wondered what would befall us. I hid my tears and denied my fears for that was how men handled times of great travail. With both of us caught in the grip of melancholia, though, the day came when we were weary beyond measure. Physically and emotionally spent, our goal lay far beyond our reach. This trek to mountain cañons was impossible, our destination unreachable, despair the sole reality.

So I believed, until the burro brayed. Looking around, I saw nothing out of the ordinary, no threat to agitate the beast. Then I noticed Antelope Creek was clouded by muddy water. My gaze swung to Destiny.

Even though she wore a full-brimmed hat, she was sunburned. Nose peeling, her lips were cracked and bleeding. Ashes from campfires had blackened fine-boned hands, and welts from insect bites reddened a face once as smooth as porcelain. Cattle lowed in the distance. She turned, lifting her eyes to mine.

Chapter Three

The great plain was marked by a low, stone-crested ridge. At the base of the ridge a sheen reflected the midday sky. Cattle waded there, muddying the water. Destiny and I stared, both of us invigorated by the sight and scent of a natural wetland, a rarity on the prairie.

Like an ancient wall retaining a moat, the ridge backed Antelope Creek into a marshland some fifty or sixty acres in size. Fattened cattle grazed in knee-high grass amid cat-tails. The critters raised their heads, stoically observing us ford the shallow end of the marsh. Far removed from Columbine County, the Lazy 3 was a brand I had never seen before.

I studied the terrain. The creek fed the marsh on one end, and drained it on the other. In damp ground I spotted the imprints of shod hoofs. A trail veered away from the creek.

Before Destiny and I could decide whether to follow it or continue along the meandering creek, the sound of drumming hoof beats reached us. The burro shied away. Facing north, he let go with a shrill *hee-haw*. Presently we saw three riders coming at a canter.

When they drew closer, I saw three women. None rode side-saddle. Sitting Western saddles with coiled lariats, they wore divided skirts, vests over blouses, and wide-brimmed hats trailing bright ribbons.

The woman in the lead was stout, triple chinned, with her hair braided. I saw a small pistol in a holster around her ample waist. When the trio closed in on us, she brandished the gun. They reined up, amazement registering in their faces. A moment passed before they recovered and fired off a volley of questions.

"What are you children doing here?"
"Where's your folks?"
"Where on earth did you come from?"
"Are you children alone?"

The stout woman holstered her gun. "Well?"

I began: "My name is Michael, and this is my brother Joe. . . ."

Before I could launch into our rehearsed tale, the second woman gestured vigorously at Destiny.

"That's no he!"

I turned to her. The woman was rail thin, her facial features hawk-like as she studied us. Destiny eyed her, offering no reply.

The third woman nodded agreement. "You're a girl. Aren't you, honey?"

A yellow ribbon was tied around the crown of her blue hat. Her vest and skirt were blue, too. Sporting brass buttons, with a saber she could have passed for cavalry.

The second woman announced tersely: "Runaways."

When we did not respond immediately, the stocky woman turned to me. "Did you kidnap this little girl?"

Destiny came to my defense until the stocky woman cut her off. "Tell the truth," she said. "Are you children runaways, or not?"

Destiny and I exchanged a glance. She nodded once.

Thus, our introduction to the proprietors of the Lazy 3 cattle ranch. Gladys packed a pistol, Violet was thin, Orchid wore blue. The Quincy sisters were anything but lazy. We soon learned they were industrious. Whether filling the root cellar, making cheeses, or carding and spinning wool, they came as close to a state of self-sufficiency on the Colorado prairie as anyone I had ever known.

As I later learned, they rarely allowed a male on the place. With an exception or two, *man*power was not needed. The sisters stayed together every day, partly for self-protection, partly to demonstrate their readiness to face any task, to conquer any adversary. Up until the day we met them, "rancher" in my vocabulary meant "man." It did not take long for me to expand my definition of the term.

The log ranch house and horse barn were tidy, roof lines straight. Pansies bloomed in window boxes, and potted geraniums lined a footpath to the steps of the front porch. Outbuildings were white-washed, weeds and wild grasses trimmed, fences up. My father often stated his conviction that the condition of fencing on a place took the measure of the farmer or stockman.

"Fences slack, so is the man," he used to say.

I looked around the Lazy 3 Ranch headquarters, taking it all in. Father would have approved. Secured with chicken wire to discourage rabbits and deer, the sisters' garden plots were loaded with vegetables. Beyond it, coops housed a menagerie of chickens, ducks, and turkeys. Sturdy pens protected them, and sheds held milk cows in addition to goats and sheep. Half a dozen ranch dogs, assigned to predator control and moon howling, took turns sniffing my pants leg, tails slowly wagging. That task completed, they headed for shade beside the house—all but one.

He was big, a male mastiff perhaps tipping the scales at 120 pounds. He trailed after me and held close as I tended the burro. I looked at him and he looked at me. I bent down and petted him. Broad through his shoulders and narrow at the hips, he was a fine specimen of a powerful breed. Short-haired, his coat was the color of a fawn, his blunt snout black as coal. With brow furrowed, he watched me drape panniers over the top rail of the corral.

Destiny had been assisted indoors by Violet and Orchid. Her knees were weak, and the two sisters supported her on either side as they slowly mounted four steps and crossed the porch. I lost sight of her when they entered the house. Later, I learned Destiny had bathed and been slathered from head to toe with high-smelling ointments. According to the sisters, "medicinal oils" took the sting out of sunburns and hastened the healing of "angrified" insect bites.

The armed sister, Gladys, marched me to a small cabin beyond the barn and corral. We were fol-lowed by the mastiff until she suddenly turned and kicked dirt in his face. Wheeling, the dog trotted away, vigorously shaking his head.

"Worthless mutt," she said after him. "I don't know why I keep him on the place. I paid top dollar to a cowhand who claimed he's trained. Supposed to be a fighting dog, but he's scared of his own shadow." She turned to me. "Bunk here."

Dirt floored and windowless, the cabin was furnished with two narrow bunks and a bucket, nothing more—no straw or cotton mattress, no blanket, no chair or stool, not even a peg to hang a hat. If the message was unclear, needlepoint script tacked on the wall spelled it out for drifters and itinerant ranch hands who could read.

Take No Comfort Here
Bucko
For Tomorrow You Shall Ride

The cabin was occupied seasonally, Gladys explained, by a pair of cowhands hired to brand, castrate, and de-horn Lazy 3 livestock. Then, in the autumn, hired hands made a gather of four-year-olds. They left a man behind as caretaker, and drove the cattle to the railroad spur. The sisters negotiated a deal with a buyer from the stockyards, and, after paying off the hired men, they divided profits three ways.

In their annual trip by rail to Chicago, they visited the First National Bank and deposited a share of their profits. From there they proceeded to spend money in elegant hotels and fine restaurants, attended operas, plays, and all of the cultural events they hungered for eleven months out of the year. Those dramas and chorus-line shows would be discussed in detail while the sisters were housebound on winter days, or seeking shade on hot summer evenings. While in the city they restocked. Purchasing fabric, notions, and various oils, they returned to the home ranch where they paid the caretaker and sent him on his way.

Gladys thrust a towel and a jar of ointment at me. Opening the jar, I winced. Castor oil stirred into vinegar-laced lard was an evil-smelling concoction. If strong odors signaled healing powers, then this one was sure-fire. Gladys waved toward the horse trough at the corral.

"Climb in," she said, "and scrub thoroughly."

When I did not make a move to comply, she impatiently waved her hand at me. "Go on. Strip. Strip and get in there."

I took offense. Destiny and I were not infested with lice or fleas or any other vermin. I looked her in the eye and described our bathing routine on the trail.

Turtle-like, Gladys drew her chin into folds of flesh. "You will not be allowed within a hundred feet of my sisters or that young girl. Not until you have bathed properly. Not until you have deloused."

I shook my head while she glowered.

"I shall stand here and see that you do," she said. "Now, peel down. Strip to the skin, and be quick about it. I have work to do."

I shook my head once.

Gladys nodded twice.

Observed by milling dogs and by Gladys herself, I took off my clothes, underwear and all. Removing my eyeglasses, I threw a leg over the edge of the trough and lowered myself, feet first, into scummy water. Laced with algae, the water was remarkably cold. Without warning, Gladys reached out and pushed my head under. She held me there for the longest fifteen seconds of my life. I came up blowing and sputtering.

Goose-bumped and naked as a jaybird, I climbed out and hurriedly smeared the stinking ointment on my skin while Gladys looked on. She pointed out places I had missed. Gladys herself was not one to miss anything. For her, no body parts were private.

From the first moments of our acquaintanceship, the sisters had seen through our little ruse. We did not even have a chance to spin our yarn about the horrible death of our mother in a fire. By the time I was permitted entry into the ranch house, Destiny had been revived by her bath and satiated with a bowl of hot soup with cheese and crackers.

I went in with Gladys. The moment Destiny and I looked at one another, I sensed she had told all.

I looked around. L-shaped with bedrooms down the hall, the house was spacious. In the front room, log walls had been covered with boards, and the flat surface wallpapered. A pattern of vines twisted through large green leaves. The room itself was furnished with cushioned armchairs and upholstered fainting couches. No arm or back lacked for a lace doily, and every pillow was fringed and tasseled to a fair-thee-well. Ornately framed landscapes and romanticized pastoral scenes hung from the walls. Flanking the door, glassed bookcases held thick, leather-bound volumes—*The Complete Works of William Shakespeare* and the modestly titled *Encyclopedic History of the Modern World* among them.

Violet and Orchid turned in their chairs and took their measure of me. Orchid demanded to know who I was and where I had come from. My sense was they merely wanted to compare my version with the account they had heard from Destiny.

I thought about how much I would reveal while Gladys edged in close behind me. A gust of her breath wafted over the back of my neck.

"The truth, this time," she said.

I discovered a truism: it is difficult, if not impossible, to lie in the presence of a woman who has seen you naked. I gave the sisters an accurate account of our trek, truncated as it was, and in the end they seemed satisfied with my version.

I had long considered my father to be a taskmaster. I soon learned he took a back seat to the Quincy sisters. After a day of rest, they piled on the chores. First, I was ordered to scrub my clothes. Rinsed and wrung out, I hung each garment on a line of cotton rope to dry in the sun.

Gladys inspected them for cleanliness. Rejects were tossed into the dirt at my feet.

"Don't be a weak pup," she said. "Put some muscle into the job."

I felt anger building while I scrubbed fabric on the ribbed washboard of galvanized steel. From a safe distance, the mastiff stretched out on the ground, watching me with brow knitted as though trying to comprehend what the hell was happening here. In truth, so was I.

Then came chores around the home place. Except for milking, separating cream, churning butter, and weeding garden plots, most of the tasks involved the clean-up of animal droppings and laying down beds of clean straw—the repetitive, endless tasks all too familiar to a farm boy. The chief difference from home to here was that these chores were imposed with at least one sister standing by, eyes fixed on me to make certain Quincy standards were met. I figured those standards had been elevated. I worked hard for long hours, dawn to dark, all the while wondering how the sisters had kept up with chores before I came along.

I suspected they were merely trying to run me off the place. My suspicion grew when they heaped more jobs on me and uttered increasingly stern criticisms. Nothing I did was good enough. It occurred to me that I could leave any time I wished, and perhaps they were shoving me in that direction. Even though I was clean and high-smelling, measuring up to the Quincy standard of perfection, I was handed meals out the back door. I ate while kneeling on the stoop like a saddle tramp.

The mastiff followed me, snarling at other ranch dogs that wandered too close to me. Against orders from Gladys, I fed the big dog out of my hand. After that, he rarely let me out of his sight. Lying at my feet in the cabin, he alternately dozed and gazed at me, that brow knitted in a perpetual query.

Petting him, I tried to think of a name. Father believed dogs routinely killed chickens, ate eggs, trampled gardens, and fled from coyotes and foxes. He had never allowed a dog on the place, so I lacked experience in this area of common knowledge.

With the mastiff, my habit had been to say—"Here, boy."—when I fed him. In time it was shortened to a whispered: "Boy." He responded to it, tail wagging. Not much of a name, but it stuck.

The mastiff was smart. He demonstrated intelligence merely by nosing the cabin door open at daybreak. He knew he was not supposed to be there. Every morning Gladys stepped out on the verandah to call me to breakfast at the back door. By then the mastiff was gone. She never figured out her worthless mutt was a step ahead of her.

I rarely saw Destiny, and I hankered for her. She stayed in the ranch house most of the time. Once we happened to meet as she came out of the outhouse. Rushing to one another, we clasped hands. Before we could talk, Violet came for her.

Solicitously grasping a thin arm, she ushered Destiny to the house as though escorting an infirm patient into a sanatorium.

I offered to visit, but I was told Destiny was still recovering from her ordeal. She needed more rest, Gladys informed me in a tone that left no room for discussion, and she needed more time to benefit from a healthful diet. In truth, I did not doubt the validity of the sisters' concern. I figured Destiny needed prolonged rest. She needed that, along with the rich diet of eggs, buttermilk, oatmeal, cornbread or fritters, and soft cheese provided by the Quincy sisters.

Upon learning they were vegetarians, I thought of Mr. Porter and his nose for hypocrisy. I figured he would thrust his verbal rapier into the heart of numerous contradictions here. Beginning with eating unborn chickens for breakfast every morning, and continuing with the fact that animals were slain and their hides tanned for use in leather shoes, belts, the saddles they sat, and the reins they held. Icky would no doubt have concluded the debate with a tally of profits from the sale of Lazy 3 steers destined for the slaughterhouse.

I did not raise the issue for debate. No point, I figured, in further antagonizing the sisters.

As the days wore on, I became convinced they were bent on pushing me away, on separating Destiny from me. In reply to my repeated offers to visit, I was informed she was resting, busy with kitchen chores, or practicing sewing skills. She could not be disturbed by the likes of me.

After three weeks of this treatment, Jennings anger boiled over. I demanded to see Destiny. I figured she was keen to see me, too, and said as much to Gladys. Her authority challenged, she tucked in her chin, exposing pimples in creases between sweaty rolls of flesh at her throat.

"In due time, Michael," she said, "after the child has fully regained her strength. For now, if you wish to remain on our ranch and eat our food, you must perform chores. Above all, you must obey grown-ups. Fail to do either, and you will have to leave. Do you understand?"

I understood. The Quincy sisters were trying to break us up. I did not understand why.

The question plagued me day and night. I lost sleep thinking about it. I kept reviewing that encounter with Gladys, thinking of all the should-have-saids. The more I thought about it, the more my emotions churned. What right did she have to order me around? What right did she have to determine the course of Destiny's life?

Sleeplessness drove me out of the cabin at night. Trailed by the mastiff, my habit was to walk around the barn and corral, sometimes venturing across grasslands by starlight. From a distance the barn loomed like a great shadow in the star-studded sky. Beyond it, lamplight glowed from ranch house windows.

One night I spooked an owl. The sudden flutter of wings startled me, and I drew back as though I had been jumped by some nocturnal predator. Boy growled, and I gave him a pat on the head. I circled the ranch house, drawn closer by the light cast through small windowpanes. Curtains were partly open.

Like an eavesdropper, I watched the sisters don long flannel nightgowns and wash from porcelain basins as they prepared to turn in for the night. Gladys occupied the first bedroom. I caught a glimpse of her placing her pistol next to her pillow before she blew out the lamp. In the next bedroom Orchid vigorously combed her hair before an oval mirror on her bureau. Destiny had been given a folding cot in Violet's room at the end of the hallway.

I paused there. Destiny sat cross-legged on the cot, dressed in a borrowed nightgown. I saw her reading aloud from a hefty, leather-bound volume propped up on her crossed legs.

As her voice drifted to me, memories surged. I was reminded of recitations in school. Mr. Porter had been dead wrong in his admonition. Destiny did not need to speak louder. Her soft voice cut deep. Not since leaving home had I felt such pangs of loneliness as I did in those moments of observing her through that window.

I pulled away. I had not expected to weep. Boy leaned against me. At that moment I felt separated from Destiny by a wide gulf. Boy followed me back to the cabin, staying close enough to bump against my leg as I hurried along. For a reason I could not fully identify, his presence was a comfort to me.

In the darkness of the cabin, schemes of counterattack swirled through my mind. Such fantasies involved kicking a door open—outdistancing three enraged sisters in mad pursuit—fleeing for our lives with the burro—all of us running at full tilt.

In truth, I did not possess the fortitude to challenge the sisters. They were adults. By the standards of my upbringing, grown-ups were in charge. Unquestioning obedience was the child's rôle. Heavy-handed as he was, Father had pounded his version of respect into me, and here, on their ranch, I figured the Quincy sisters held all the cards.

Yet I knew I had to talk to Destiny—privately. Somehow.

On a starry night after household lamps were extinguished, I waited outside the darkened window to Violet's room. I passed the time by petting Boy. Then I stood. Drawing a deep breath, I leaned close to the window and tapped on a pane. No response. I waited. Drew another deep breath. Tapped again. I figured Destiny would not awaken unless I made a louder sound—and risked awakening Violet.

The curtains moved and slowly parted. I adjusted my eyeglasses. Peering through the lenses, I half expected to see Violet's aquiline nose and raptorial eyes on the other side of the glass. But it was Destiny who pressed her hands to the dark panes. She motioned to me, jabbing her index finger toward the front door.

I backed away from the window and stumbled over Boy. He lunged and bumped against me as though playing a game. Catching my balance, I turned and hurried toward the front of the house. Boy loped along with me in his easy pace. I rounded the corner and halted at the verandah steps. A long moment passed before the door eased open. Destiny came out.

We held hands as we gazed at one another by starlight. I was keen to tell her how much I missed her, but the words jammed up on me. Tail wagging, Boy tried to crowd in between us. I leaned down and shoved him away. He took it for play, and came back for more. Without thinking, I ordered him to sit. Boy promptly obeyed. Tail wagging, he looked up at me as though awaiting further instructions. When I said—"Down."—he went down and rested his chin on his front paws, tail still wagging.

I heard Destiny's voice, her words coming to me in a soft whisper.

"Michael, I . . . I am frightened . . . so frightened."

"Are you all right?"

"No."

"What's wrong?"

"Gladys . . . Gladys told me. . . ."

"Told you what?"

"She told me . . . told me you wanted to be left alone."

"Alone?"

"She told me you were going back to Columbia. Michael, I have to stay here . . . for now."

"I never said that."

"What?"

"I'm not going back."

"You're not?"

"I never said I was. Not to Gladys. Not to anyone."

I saw Destiny's upturned face bathed in starlight. We gazed at one another, momentarily silenced by the realization that an adult had lied. She moved closer and wrapped her arms around me. We held one another. I felt the soft warmth of her body pressing against me. Shuddering, she wept again. In the ranch house a floorboard creaked. Boy fled when the door opened.

Violet came out, easing into starlight. Barefooted, she wore a long, white nightgown. A gentler spirit than Gladys, she was no shrinking violet, either.

"What are you doing," she demanded. "Sneaking around in the middle of the night?"

When she was answered by our silence, she accused me of luring Destiny in a plot to run away. Another false accusation from an adult sent a wave of hot anger surging through me. Like it or not, I am my father's son, and my temper erupted.

70

"Gladys lied about me!"

Violet studied me. "What are you carrying on about?"

"She told Destiny I was leaving!"

"Perhaps you should," Violet said evenly. "You certainly have no right to endanger the life of a twelve-year-old girl."

Destiny started to protest, but Violet swiftly silenced her.

"After you have had time to think about it," Violet said, "you will understand what he's up to."

"I'm not up to anything," I said.

I was eager to defend myself, but at once uncertain of her meaning. The workings of the world, including a knowledge of carnal desires, were lost on me.

Destiny came to my defense. "We traveled together all the way from Columbia. We're trying to find my pa. I told you."

"That's the truth," I said. Struggling against mounting anger, I repeated: "Gladys lied about me. . . ."

I was distracted by the sight of a wide shadow moving into the doorway behind Violet.

"What's the ruckus all about?" Gladys demanded.

Wearing a nightgown like a ship's sail, she appeared before us with Orchid a pace behind. Shadows were set in motion as Orchid stepped onto the verandah carrying a candle in a brass holder. By the light of the flame, I saw the pistol clenched in Gladys's hand.

Destiny moved to my side. "We were talking."

"Talking," Gladys repeated with a note of sarcasm. "What about?"

"Telling the truth," I said.

Gladys swiftly turned her attention to me. "What is that supposed to mean?"

"You said I had to tell the truth," I said. "But you're the one who lied. You lied about me."

"If you mean did I protect Destiny while looking out for her best interests, then yes, of course, I did. . . ."

"I don't need your protection," Destiny broke in.

"Yes, you do," Gladys said, waving the gun to emphasize her point. "Oh, yes, you do." She drew a breath. "You may not know it, young lady, but this boy has poisoned your mind. He has poisoned you with impure thoughts."

"No, he hasn't," Destiny said.

"When you're older, you'll understand," Gladys said. "And you'll thank me."

Violet spoke to her sisters in a theatrical *sotto voce*. "Running away was the topic of the evening, I believe."

"I'm not surprised," Gladys said, glowering for my benefit.

Destiny said: "You can't make us stay here."

Gladys advanced a pace toward her. "Oh, can't I?"

"I told you," Destiny said, "we have to find my pa."

"You'll need a sight more help than you will ever get from this boy," Gladys said. She jabbed the revolver at me. "Destiny, he was nearly the death of you. We saved your life. Have you forgotten that?"

Destiny grew still, her gaze fixed on the pistol.

Despite the superheated anger of the moment, I did not feel intimidated by the gun. Waved in my direction, the hammer was down. I figured Gladys was largely unaware of it, that she might as well have poked a quill pen at me as a means of underscoring her accusations.

By candlelight I saw Destiny glance at me. She bowed her head, striking a pose of humility.

"No, ma'am, I din't forget," she said quietly. "You have been kind to me. All three of you."

"All right, then," Gladys said. She spoke to Destiny in a falsetto voice, as though summoning a favorite pet. "Come along. Time for bed. Come along, now."

I watched Destiny cross the verandah to the door. She did not look at me. Over her shoulder, Gladys spoke to me in a dismissive tone of voice as though she had prevailed in our dispute.

"Return to your bunk, Michael. If further discussion of this subject is required, we shall take it up in the morning."

I could have argued. But Destiny's pose and her meek tone of voice signaled me. She was not one to give in easily, yet she just had. If I divined the message from her change of attitude, then this was not the time to swap threats or defy the Quincy sisters.

I headed for the cabin. Boy picked me up on the way. When I opened the cabin door, the dog pranced in. I followed, and closed the door. In near darkness Boy rested his chin on the edge of the bunk. I was aware he waited until I had pulled off my boots to flop down on the floor for the night.

Unable to sleep, I lay awake for a long time. I thought about what I should have said and what I should have done during the confrontation with the sisters. As to the argument, I was not certain who had carried the day, but I was certain I had read Destiny's unspoken message. Later that night, I was proven to be correct.

I was asleep when Boy whined. Moments later I heard a *tap-tap* on the door. I left the bunk and opened it.

"Michael, my burro's gone."

Destiny's hushed voice came out of midnight darkness.

"Burro," I repeated.

"They took him somewhere," she said. She drew a deep breath. "That's how they'll keep us here. I heard them talking."

Either sleep fogged my brain, or she spoke in a disjointed manner. "What?"

"They were talking about the county sheriff," Destiny explained. "A deputy makes the rounds of the ranches every month or so. He'll be here in a week or ten days if he's on schedule."

Even in the darkness I knew Destiny was upset. She breathed hard, her voice taut. By starlight coming through the doorway, we gazed at one another. For me, the significance of it all sank in. I went to the bunk, found my boots, and pulled them on.

"I'll find him."

"How?" she asked.

"He has to be around here somewhere."

"Michael."

I stood and faced her. She grasped my arm with both hands.

"Those mean things Gladys said about you. . . ." Destiny's voice trailed off. "Michael, I know she's wrong. You helped me. You've helped me every day since we left Columbia. I couldn't have made it this far without you. I know that . . . even if I din't ever tell you. I couldn't stand it, the way Gladys talked about you." She paused again. "Michael, if you want to take your own trail. . . ."

I asked: "Do you still want to find out what happened to your father?"

She nodded.

"So do I," I said.

Destiny stepped into my embrace, and we held one another. Parting, I watched her stride away, hurrying to the ranch house. When she let herself in, I left the cabin with Boy at my heels.

Chores had kept me busy since our arrival, and in truth I had not given a thought to the burro. Destiny was right. Without that gray, long-eared beast, we were trapped, forced to stay on the Lazy 3 Ranch property until the lawman arrived.

Boy surged ahead of me, circled, and came back. I went to the corral and found it empty. I entered the barn. Working by feel in darkness, I touched saddle mounts in their stalls. No long-eared boarders were present among the horses. After a search of the sheds and the second corral, an idea came to me.

I remembered a path leading through prairie grass and around clumps of sage. It led away from the barn to open prairie. I found the path by the light of stars. From there, I merely followed Boy.

The well-worn footpath angled away from the marsh and topped a rise half a mile away from the barn and pole corrals. On the far side of the rise, Boy led me to a shed and fenced enclosure. In the dim starlight I made out blackened circles on the ground—gray ashes and charred embers left by branding fires. Beyond the shed a herd of steers were bunched in an old buffalo wallow. Hobbled, the mouse-gray burro stood among them. His long ears twitched when he spotted me.

I made a quick search of the shed. My hands probed loose hay on the floor, and my fingers touched leather and wicker panniers—Destiny's packs.

I thought about what to do next. I decided to

leave them here, covered, and to leave the burro, too.

With the mastiff loping ahead, I jogged back to ranch headquarters. My thoughts raced. I considered awakening Destiny, but thought better of it. Tomorrow I would talk to her—with or without permission.

Summoned in the morning by the customary shout from Gladys, I took breakfast on the back stoop. I lingered, keeping an eye out for Destiny. When she stepped into the kitchen, I gestured through the window. She crossed the room, opened the back door, and leaned out.

She was elated when I whispered the location of her burro and the packs. Then and there we agreed. The time had come. Destiny pulled away. She closed the door, retreating when Violet entered the kitchen.

Our plan was simple. Destiny would inform the sisters of our departure. No matter what came next—an array of arguments or a torrent of tears—she would be ready when I came for her with the burro in tow.

Followed by Boy, I left the ranch house. I headed for the path leading past the barn and across the prairie. On the way I wooled over everything that could possibly go wrong. I figured the sisters would persuade and dissuade, threaten and cajole, and finally demand obedience from Destiny as a means of repaying the debt she owed them for saving her life. Among all the possibilities, I never doubted she would stand firm.

I jogged past the barn, and hit my stride as I ran hard along the path. Boy liked this game. The big mastiff plunged ahead, tongue out, tail up as we raced. He won easily.

In the morning nothing went wrong. The burro was still there. So were the panniers and lead rope under the hay. After positioning the thick blanket, I hefted the panniers on the burro's back. I removed the hobbles and led him back to the cabin. Under Boy's watchful eyes, I gathered up my belongings. Then I headed for the ranch house with the dog close at my heels.

Rounding the corner of the barn, I looked ahead. Destiny stood on the edge of the verandah, alone, dressed in her father's altered duds. From all outward appearances, she could have been awaiting the arrival of a coach at some remote station.

I saw folded clothing under one arm—garments sewn under the supervision of Violet and Orchid, I figured. I did not know if the Quincy sisters had underestimated Destiny's resolve, but when I saw her standing there, a solitary figure on the verandah, I knew she had proven the point she had uttered last night.

You can't make us stay here.

The sisters must have been forced to acknowledge that fact. No one could deny the larger truth—namely, if we did not depart in broad daylight, we would merely slip away some night while they slept.

Gladys stepped out through the door. Head bowed in solemnity, she crossed the porch like a queen in defeat. She was followed by Violet and Orchid. All three women moved in a slow, funereal march as Destiny descended the steps ahead of them.

"You will regret this decision," Gladys said. "Forever."

Violet and Orchid looked on. I figured they knew the dispute was finished, that all of the pronouncements had been pronounced, that further argument was fruitless. They had accepted the verdict, even if Gladys had not.

Destiny halted on the bottom step. She turned and gazed up at the three sisters, standing side-by-side. When she spoke softly, I recognized a quotation from the repertoire of Mr. Porter himself.

" 'Forever is time without end,' " she recited. " 'Can mere mortals comprehend?' "

As highfalutin as the quotation was, Gladys vigorously shook her head, blithely unaware that she had dared dismiss the wisdom of Ichabod. Destiny turned away.

Descending the last step, she moved to the burro and opened a pannier. She put the articles of clothing inside. I caught a glimpse of Violet. The slight woman turned and rushed into the house through the open door. Returning moments later, she lugged a cloth sack.

Violet moved past her sisters and hurried down the steps. She thrust the sack out to Destiny, and ventured a quick smile. Destiny accepted it. I watched while she opened it and peered in.

"Oh, thank you," Destiny murmured, and lifted her gaze to Violet. "Thank you very much."

Violet turned and mounted the steps. Gladys averted her eyes, but Orchid smiled as she looked on.

Destiny put the sack in a pannier while I held the lead rope taut. I mumbled my gratitude to the three sisters for the food and shelter they had provided. Gladys ignored me, no doubt still believing Destiny was trapped in my evil orbit, that I bore responsibility for her defiance.

Perhaps my words rang hollow. The sisters may well have heard a lack of sincerity in my voice. In truth, I figured they should have thanked me for the work I had completed on their place. Working without complaint or pay, I had performed every chore asked of me.

For her part, Gladys uttered one last directive. "I've seen that mutt sticking to you like glue. Don't think I haven't seen you hand-feeding him . . . against my orders."

I looked at Boy. His tail wagged.

Destiny spoke up. "Ma'am, if there was some

way we could buy the dog, I have four dollars and seventy cents. . . ."

Gladys shook her head. "He's a ranch dog, and here he stays."

The offer from Destiny surprised me. That specific amount was familiar to me. I had not known until then that she carried the money found on the corpse identified as her father.

My gaze shifted from her to Gladys. I think we both knew she had no real interest in the dog. She wielded ownership of Boy as a means of punishing me for undermining her authority with Destiny.

"Shut him up in the barn," Gladys said curtly. "Shut him in there, and close the door. Then you may leave our ranch."

I knew I had no choice as I looked at the dog. He looked at me, dark brown eyes slowly blinking. I drew a breath. Better get this done quickly, I figured.

"Boy," I whispered, and headed for the horse barn.

The mastiff leaped to his feet. He loped ahead when he saw where I was going. Reaching the barn, I pulled the outsize door open. Boy pranced in. A hinge squealed as I pushed the door. Boy spun around. Too late, he lunged toward me in a break for daylight. I closed the door before he got there.

I heard Boy whine, his claws scratching the inside of the door. He yelped. Fighting tears, I strode back to the verandah where Destiny waited.

I shoved my eyeglasses into place. Above all, I did not want to give Gladys the satisfaction of seeing me weep.

After voicing hollow good byes, Destiny and I walked away from the ranch house and tidy out-buildings. The burro followed, kicking up his hoofs as though demonstrating his eagerness to leave this place. More likely, he was trying to shed the pan-niers. He soon gave up the effort and settled into a walk as he brought up the rear.

In a glance back, I saw the Quincy sisters. Gladys, Orchid, and Violet stood on their verandah looking after us, a tableau fraught with meaning if there ever was one.

My gaze went to Destiny at my side. She tugged her broad-brimmed hat, now decorated with a yellow ribbon. Eyes blinking rapidly, she did not look back.

Chapter Four

Count me among those who do not believe mere mortals are prescient—my conviction so stated after years of study, contemplation, of day and night dreaming. We do not know how things are going to wind up, not until the moment passes and we look back to see time refracted through the prism of experience.

Having stated my position, though, I admit Destiny called it right. She speculated I would pursue a career in academia—a professor, she pre-dicted in the course of that awkward conversation of ours so long ago.

In truth, I graduated from the University of Chicago and went on to earn a post-graduate degree from that institution of higher learning. Later, when I was offered a position, I joined the faculty at Northwestern University in Evanston, Illinois, and settled into the land of Lincoln for the duration of my career.

As "Prof," I delivered lectures to two generations of students. My field of study evolved and finally came to be labeled "Social Sciences." By any name, a lengthy and rewarding teaching career kept the wolf from my door, as they say, while I married and raised a family consisting of two strapping sons, Ethan and Richard, and one beautiful daughter, Emily Jane. Among our adventures as a family over the years were three trips to Europe where I lectured and toured the region.

Successful.

Inspirational.

Exemplary.

These three descriptive terms were my accolades. Students and fellow professors alike bestowed them upon me at retirement. I accepted with pride in a ceremony and dinner hosted by the president, provost, and a squad of deans. To this day, as pro-fessor emeritus, I treasure those three words and feel humbled by their assignation to my life and career. Yet, in truth, during all of those years behind a podium in a lecture hall or seated at my desk in my office on campus, I yearned for something else. I wanted to be a poet.

My deepest passion was to discover the right words while creating verses in all of the classical genres. In time, though, I was forced to admit my poems neither soared nor enlightened. The muse never visited me, much less sang. As a noted academician once informed me: "Appreciators can never be creators, and good diction with a predilection for alliteration does not make a poet."

That comment, casually tossed off as it was, represented a great truth that I battled for years. At last I bowed to unassailable wisdom. I came to accept the fact that I was consigned to a reader's life of wonderment and admiration of the literary arts—even awe—but on the outside looking in, always.

I recognized great poetry and admired fine verse without ever penning a single memorable line myself. I still compose. But like the tone-deaf musician, the lines are for my amusement. Better than anyone, I know my couplets and quatrains are stiff as lumber, my stanzas heavy as lead, my meter dull as stone, my similes lame.

I know all of that to be true, just as I know that only once in my life did I walk with Destiny.

Leaving the Lazy 3 Ranch that sun-soaked morning, we skirted the marsh and resumed our trek along the banks of Antelope Creek. In our westward course, we walked at a slow pace to conserve energy and to limit blistering on our feet. Resting often, we pulled off our boots and socks to plunge bare feet into the water.

I observed Destiny as she reclined on her elbows with bare feet submerged in gentle currents. She eyed moving water as though lulled by it, and wondered aloud if the Quincy sisters would hit the saddles and ride after us. Would they make one last attempt to confine us until the deputy sheriff came and took us into custody?

She smiled when I reminded her that she had expressed similar concerns about Noah Locke. No, I did not think the sisters would come galloping after us like misguided rescuers chasing Destiny. Gladys had made her pronouncement, scowled and growled, all but ordering us off the ranch, banished, never to return. Gladys Quincy was not a woman to back down from her ultimatums. That was how I had her pegged, anyway.

Destiny dried her feet and pulled on her father's heavy socks. She retrieved the sack Violet had given her, and took out the contents one by one. Among put-up vegetables in jars sealed by wax, and soft cheeses wrapped in cloth, she found matches in a watertight holder. Cylindrical, the brass holder bore her initials—VQ—engraved in an elaborate, calligraphic style. It was a purchase, Violet had told Destiny earlier, made in Chicago several years ago. Violet had not told Destiny it would be a gift. She must have made a mental note when Destiny admitted that she had forgotten to bring matches.

Now Destiny gazed at it. Eyes closing, she drew it to her chest as though receiving jewelry to be treasured.

I thought about the sisters. I still harbored a full measure of anger toward them, Gladys in particular. Even so, I had to confess they were an interesting bunch. Of the three, Violet was the quiet one—compassionate, yet forceful in her own quiet way. She was, I supposed, a woman guided by instinct more than reason. Or by prescience?

When I thought more about it, I realized Violet had not had enough time to gather up all the items in that sack while she left the verandah and dashed into the ranch house. She must have filled it earlier, and added the watertight container from her possessions. That meant she knew—or shrewdly guessed—her sister Gladys would come out on the losing end of the dispute with Destiny. In the end, *you can't make us stay here* was a dictum, one to be heeded by caretakers, parents, jailers.

I figured Violet could not bear to cast two "children" out on the wild prairie with only the grub lugged all the way from Columbia on the back of a burro. In anticipation of that prospect, she had filled a sack of goods last night or early this morning. By presenting it upon the very moment of

86

our departure, she preëmpted Gladys, a *fait accompli*, and thus averted an argument.

That first night away from the Quincy place I was too keyed up to sleep. All manner of memories passed through my mind. Destiny lay at my side, fast asleep. I gazed up at the bright stars of Orion in a sky as black as ink, my thoughts in freefall while I reviewed all that had happened in the last several weeks. I also remembered one of Ichabod's lessons. In the annals of Greek literature Orion was a mighty hunter. He was killed by Artemis, the virgin goddess of the hunt. I remembered Icky's spirited rendition of the tale, a story of Orion's pursuit of the Pleiades, the seven daughters of Atlas. Now with violence filling my mind while I lay under the stars, sleep crept over me—until I was suddenly awakened.

I sat up in darkness, believing I had been attacked. The side of my face felt wet. I reached to my jaw. My fingers touched moisture. Blood? This was no dream. . . .

I heard a familiar whine. Suddenly I knew. Extending my hand into darkness, I touched hide and hair. Leaning forward, I came nose to snout with the mastiff.

Boy licked my face again.

Destiny and I crossed the empty plain with the big dog bounding ahead and the burdened burro following. An odd little caravan, we would have made a strange sight had anyone been there to observe and record our passage.

We had talked about the mastiff before breaking camp. Down on his haunches while we spoke, Boy watched with brow knitted, as though sensing his fate was under discussion.

In truth, Destiny and I never gave serious consideration to returning him to the Lazy 3. We did not want to backtrack all that way, any more than we wished to renew our dispute with the sisters three. Nor did I have the heart to pitch stones at the dog to drive him away. I remembered Gladys had kicked dirt in his face, and figured he had reason to run off. Now that the mastiff had managed to escape confinement and throw in with us, returning him to the ranch would have amounted to an act of cruelty. Such was my rationale for the theft of a good dog.

Opening my pocketknife, I sliced bite-sized chunks of jerky, and pushed Boy away while I soaked them in water. Tail swinging back and forth, he ate the softened meat with energetic chewing and a great deal of slobbering. Destiny laughed while she watched him.

Every day when we set out, Boy trotted ahead. He frequently looked back to make sure we were coming along. To the west, mountains appeared on the pale horizon like a convoy of ships traversing a dark, distant sea. How many miles separated us from the peaks and cañons was unknown to me. I had never been close to a mountain range before, much less climbed a peak.

Over the next several days Destiny and I became aware of a swifter current in Antelope Creek. The water was colder, too, quickly numbing our bare feet. We left wild grasses and thick stands of rabbit-brush behind as we began our ascent to higher altitudes. Foothills were marked by pear cactus and thin grasses. Farther west, the hills divided the creek into small, rushing tributaries. We stayed with the largest one, following it upstream. Four days later we entered a wide cañon.

Pines grew tall, straight as spears from a giant's arsenal. Left and right I saw prospect holes dotting the cañon walls at higher elevations. Miners had been here—been and gone. With no sight or sounds of animals, and no scent of smoke from campfires, the mine sites were clearly abandoned.

Hand-drilled and blasted out by prospectors in search of ore, each bore was marked by oxidized tailings. In the parlance of the trade, tailings consisted of loosened material shoveled from the earth—rock and soil undisturbed since the age of glaciers. Oxidized by moisture from snow and rain, the tailings turned to a rusty, yellow-red-orange color like scabbed wounds.

As I learned from later research, each prospect hole started where outcroppings had held promise to some miner's eye. Dreams of wealth spurred these men. They kept searching and digging, even though precious few possessed practical knowledge of locating mineral deposits. Their boreholes were merely stabs in the dark, each one abandoned, each one representing failure.

Digging out small tunnels or sinking shallow shafts were the only exploratory techniques available to hard-rock miners of the era. Every prospector's dream was to uncover a vein near the surface—easy diggings as they say. Tales of burros kicking over a rock to expose a deposit of gold or silver ore abounded. Most miners relied on horseshit luck when it came to the realities of locating a vein. Trained geologists, it was claimed, had missed deposits later discovered by an ignorant prospector chasing his runaway burro, or by an intoxicated prospector falling down only to awaken later to find ore staring him in the face. Whether the yarns were true or not, the goal was to remove just enough country rock to expose an ore body. Claimed, assayed, and registered, then, the site could be worked by the discoverer, or sold.

Destiny and I discovered the open prairie was far easier to traverse than mountainous terrain. On the prairie our line of vision stretched out for miles in any direction, allowing us to identify the easiest, shortest routes. In the mountains, cañon walls closed in. Unable to see ahead more than fifty or a hundred paces, we often backtracked when we came up against dead ends in the form of downed timber or an ancient landslide.

Our second discovery was one that should have been obvious from the start—water seeks the lowest level. A scientific principle taught by Mr. Porter, the lesson was duly memorized for the next test, and promptly forgotten. By following Antelope Creek, we moved into deeper and narrower reaches of the cañon. Game trails were left behind, a fact alone that should have alerted us.

The narrowing creek tumbled over rocks and around boulders with a dull roar. Boy still tried to lead us, scrambling over boulders. Destiny held the burro's lead rope until our passage was obstructed. Forced to admit to defeat, we turned back. Pink tongue out and breathing hard, Boy was content to follow until we returned to a wider stretch of the cañon. He bounded ahead, and, with a look back, he eagerly led the way.

We camped on a grassy flat next to a stand of white-barked aspens. The grove encircled a pond, a small body of water dammed at one end by mud and tangles of aspen branches. The perimeter was marked by pointed stumps where beavers had gnawed and dropped aspen trees with all the accuracy of a logger wielding an axe.

I heard Boy whine. The mastiff charged, running to the muddy bank of the pond. Water rippled out there. A beaver, with his nose barely above water, swam swiftly toward a mound of sticks and mud in the middle of the pond. The beaver slapped his flat tail in the water and dove to an underwater entrance of his lodge.

Boy waded to a depth that threatened to float him before he turned and dog-paddled back to us. On the bank, he shook water from his tawny coat. Destiny and I exchanged a glance, both of us smiling at the dog's antics. Boy trotted toward us, mouth open as though grinning from his futile pursuit of a member of the largest species of rodent in North America.

Too tired to gather sticks and dead wood for a fire, we ate cheese and opened two jars of fruit from the well-stocked cellar of the Quincy sisters. Hobbled, the burro fended for himself, grazing in tall, green grass. Boy explored our campsite in a widening circle. He worked his way around the meadow until I called him. He loped toward me, head up, mouth open in anticipation.

I hand-fed chunks of venison jerky to him, and, after chewing each piece, he licked my hand. Destiny laughed when Boy leaned against me. I pushed him away, and he came back for more, tail wagging in his favorite game. He responded to my command—"Sit."—and quickly obeyed—"Down." Stretched out on the ground between Destiny and me, he watched us with his ears perked. Soon his ears relaxed, his eyes closed, and he dozed.

The glassy surface of the pond was dimpled by trout rising to feed on insects. Occasionally a fish jumped, clearing the water with a splash. I glimpsed a flash of speckled skin as the native trout cleared the water.

I walked around the meadow, turning over rocks until I found earthworms. Hungry, the trout did not discriminate between a fresh hatch hovering above the water and fat earthworms writhing underwater on a barbed hook. The pond quickly yielded three deep-bellied fish.

Destiny and I cooked them over a fire. Boy sniffed as he eyed the steaming meat. I offered him a bite. He turned up his nose and walked away, clearly preferring boot-tough jerky that he chewed like a filet of rubber boot.

We spent the remainder of the day at rest. For a while I followed Boy's example, and dozed in warm sunlight. Awake, I looked around, seeing snow-crested peaks in the distance. I pondered our plight, trying to push away my fear. We were lost.

In truth, I did not know where to go from here. The only certainty in my mind was the daunting fact that the cañon was impassible. Yet miners had come this way. They must have left a road of some sort, somewhere. Had I missed it near the mouth of the cañon?

The next morning I told Destiny that I would search for a road or trail. Her lips drew together in a thin line at the prospect of being left alone. While we discussed it, Boy held close to me. A change of mood came over him. Instead of wagging his tail and investigating our campsite, he growled and grew fretful. He bared teeth at some unseen enemy. I tried to quiet him, but he growled again. Hair stood up on the back of his neck.

"What's wrong?" Destiny asked.

I adjusted my eyeglasses, and peered into the grove of aspen trees. Something was over there that held Boy's attention—or someone. When Boy growled a third time, the sound came from deep in his throat. A blue jay took wing suddenly. Two more flew away, arcing past us to show plumage matching the color of the sky.

I stood.

"What's wrong?" Destiny asked.

"Boy caught a scent."

Destiny stared at me.

"Someone's watching us," I said, and saw a look of alarm cross her face. I added: "Probably just an animal. Gone by now."

That lame theory was exploded when Boy growled again, and barked.

Eyes wide with fear, Destiny pulled on her father's boots. She scrambled to her feet, grasping my am. At once her gaze swung left and right.

"What . . . what animal? Where?"

I shrugged.

She peered into the grove. "Michael, I . . . I don't see anything."

Neither did I.

I figured Boy had detected a hostile scent. His

olfactory capabilities stretched far beyond ours. As further evidence, those blue jays had been spooked. Some creature was out there, somewhere. I was convinced of that.

When I whispered—"Boy."—the mastiff turned and came to me. "Sit." He sat on my foot, his eyes fixed on the tree line.

"Wait here," I said to Destiny. "I'll take Boy. . . ."

"Take him," she interrupted. "Take him where?"

I pointed to the stand of aspens.

"Michael . . . stay here."

I pulled free from her tight grasp. "I won't go far."

I did not know how far from our camp I had the courage to venture, but I felt emboldened by an aggressive mastiff at my command. Aware of Destiny's gaze on me, I strode away for a closer look. Boy bushwhacked ahead of me, head up. In a glance back, I saw the burro. Hobbled, he grazed contentedly where I had left him.

Destiny was anything but content. She scrambled to her feet and hurried after me.

Catching up, she grabbed my arm and held on for dear life as we approached the aspen grove. Leaves fluttered in a gentle breeze. I was watchful, at once keeping an eye on Boy for a clue to an adversary ahead. If predators roamed nearby, I figured the mastiff would react—barking or baring teeth before he attacked or retreated. Either way, I would have a warning.

Boy sniffed the ground. He seemed to be on a

trail, yet I saw no tracks in the soft earth, animal or human. No fresh droppings, either. From cool shadows cast by the trees, the grove opened to a sun-fired meadow. Wildflowers bloomed like scattered jewels, and blades of grass were bent under the weight of morning dew.

I looked past Boy. A sheer cliff loomed ahead. At its base was a low, dark shadow. Boy halted, cocking his head. The shadow was the mouth of a cave. Destiny saw it, too, and squeezed my arm with the force of a sprung trap.

Now I spotted a dim trail in the grass. The path angled toward the cave. Still, I picked up no signs of shod hoofs or the imprints of boots. No rusting cast-offs from men, either.

I pushed my eyeglasses up on my nose and moved ahead. Destiny stayed close. When we came to the cave opening, Boy suddenly plunged ahead. I called to him in a low voice, but he did not break stride.

"Boy," I said louder. "Boy!"

He disobeyed and loped into the cave, disappearing in an instant. When we drew closer, I peered in. I saw a stubby candle on the cave wall. Extinguished, the wax candle stood upright in a spiked holder. It was the type used by hard-rock miners. At a right angle to the candle, a pointed, six-inch spike had been wedged into a fissure in the stone. Reaching out, I grasped it. With a forceful tug, I pulled it free.

"Did you bring matches?"

Destiny nodded. She pulled the watertight holder bearing the initials VQ from her trouser pocket. Twisting the cylinder open, she took out a match and handed it to me.

I struck the match and held the flaring flame to the wick. When it caught, I turned to Destiny.

"Wait here."

She swallowed hard and shook her head in silent refusal.

I gazed at her. If I read her expression aright, her fear of staying here alone battled her fear of confronting a mad beast cornered in that cave. She drew a labored breath. So did I.

I knew I had to go after Boy, and pulled away from her. Holding the candle aloft then, I started after the mastiff. Darkness closed in around me. The air in the cave, cool as night, bore a strange odor. Ahead, dim shadows chased the wavering light in my outstretched hand.

Venturing deeper into the cave, the crown of my hat scraped the ceiling of granite. I bent down, and paused to look back. Crouching, Destiny came after me.

I moved ahead, slowly, aware of my heart pounding. By candlelight I saw a place where the tunnel opened a bit. I straightened up to my full height. I thought I heard a muffled sound, but I was not certain. I called the dog again.

"Boy!"

He did not come. By candlelight I saw enough detail to know that this was not a man-made tunnel shored by timbers. With no evidence of hand-drilled holes for giant powder, no burned fuses, and no tailings outside, it was clear this cave was a natural feature in the land. Recalling geography lessons in school, I figured the terrain dated back to an earlier geological era, a period countless centuries before Destiny and I trod this igneous rock solidified from a molten state.

"Boy! Boy!"

The dog did not respond to my calls. I feared for him as Destiny and I moved deeper into cool darkness. The cave angled off to our left. Rounding a bend, we halted. A chill ran up my back. The candle flame dimly illuminated an underground room, a space half the size of a horse barn. Boy was there. So was a corpse.

The gruesome sight of a hanging body took our breath away. Staring, we did not move. The corpse was white-skinned, a thick body suspended by lengths of cord anchored to the cave ceiling.

I pushed my eyeglasses up and peered at stubby legs. Boy gnawed on one of them.

Chapter Five

Cast in the wavering light of the candle flame, Destiny's face looked frozen, at once horrified and transfixed by the sight before us. Movement caught my eye. I turned and saw the corpse move when Boy bit into the flesh. He tugged at it. Growling, he pulled harder. The corpse shuddered, as though silently threatening to come back to life.

"Michael," Destiny whispered. "Oh, Michael."

Holding the candle before me, I moved closer to the corpse. I looked up. The disemboweled body was suspended by lengths of cord, each one tied to a spike driven into fissures. Knife slashes marked white flesh, some of it carved and cut away. I knew I had to get Boy away from here. I stepped toward him. Closing the distance to the corpse, I made a discovery. The object of our horror was the carcass of a bear, not a human body.

Skinned, it resembled a human corpse by candlelight. I turned to tell Destiny. I caught a glimpse of her hurrying out of the underground room. Hands to her mouth, she rushed into the cave leading outside. I turned my attention back to the dog.

"Boy. Here, Boy. Come here."

The mastiff still ignored my command. Greasy bear meat was to his strong liking. I called him again, louder, but he did not obey. I went to him. Bending down, I grasped the scruff of his neck with my free hand. Boy growled, clearly warning me.

I pulled, hard. He growled again, but finally let go of the carcass. One-handed, I needed all of my strength to pull and drag the mastiff away from his feast. He growled as he fought me, but did not snarl or try to bite. Instead, he whined as though protesting an injustice visited upon him. He lunged, trying to get away. When I spoke his name again, he turned. With a last look back at the bear carcass, he obediently followed me.

We made our way out of the underground room, and passed through the cave into bright sunlight. Destiny was there, sitting in the grass. She looked up at me, still ashen.

"Bear," I said.

She wiped her eyes with the heels of her hands. "What?"

"It's a bear," I said.

Her gaze shifted from me to the cave mouth. "Bear?"

"A hunter must have skinned it and hung it up in there," I said. "Probably to keep the meat cool."

Destiny looked around. "Is . . . is someone here?"

I shrugged. "I don't see any other signs of a hunting camp."

Destiny eyed forest shadows. If it was possible to be relieved and frightened at once, then she was. She had been relieved when I identified the bear carcass, but now she was unnerved, as though nameless creatures lurked nearby.

"Michael . . . we . . . we have to get away from this place."

I helped her stand, and we got away from that place. Boy surged ahead. We crossed the meadow and hurried through the aspen grove. Reaching our campsite, Boy yelped. He headed straight for the panniers.

Destiny and I exchanged a glance. The packs had been disturbed. One strap was unbuckled. The other pannier had been turned on its side. I heard Boy growl and saw him range left and right. Nose up, he loped to the lower edge of the grove and bulled his way through heavy brush. I heard a panicked shout.

The strained voice of someone in distress carried through the trees. I ran toward the break in the brush where I had last seen Boy. With Destiny on my heels, I passed the hobbled burro. We made our way past the pond through waist-high willows. That was where we caught up with Boy. Agitated, the mastiff looked upward. So did I. He had treed a man.

Destiny and I stared. A lightning-killed pine with bare branches and rotting bark offered refuge. Boy leaped, repeatedly yelping as he tried to bite bare feet just inches out of his range. The thought crossed my mind that he meant to complete the feast he had started in the cave—genuine human flesh this time.

I moved closer. The diminutive man who peered down at us was a foreigner.

I had never seen a man with a shaved head and pig tail before, much less an Asiatic. In truth, I had never seen a member of another race. Still growling and yelping, Boy reared up. He braced his feet against the dead tree, and scratched at the rough bark. I gave him the command to sit. He obeyed without hesitation.

Asiatic. That was the racial designation Mr. Porter used to identify the region of the world labeled by Europeans as "the Far East."

"The Asiatic race," he stated from the front of the schoolroom, "is as mysterious as the people themselves are inscrutable."

Ichabod read aloud such profoundly ignorant observations in textbooks, and he quoted excerpts from the *Travels of Marco Polo*. From school studies I had learned Marco Polo was a Venetian traveler who had led trading caravans to Asia during the late 1200s. Among his "discoveries" were paper dragons, black powder, and the manufacture of fireworks.

Mr. Porter read from *Hearns' World Traveler*: "Sallow-skinned, almond-eyed peoples of the Far East are inscrutable to the Western mind. Opium addicts engage in nefarious behaviors. The populace is sustained by bizarre diets. Travelers report eating the brains of snakes, raw, and boiling the feet of birds to brew a salty broth. The brain of any animal is considered to be a delicacy."

Such descriptive passages brought gagging

noises from Mr. Porter's students. I thought about that now as I gazed up at this man in a tree. He wore baggy black pants and a tattered gray shirt with a high collar, snug at the throat. Whether he was frightened or angry, I could not determine. I figured I was staring into the face of inscrutability, and did not know what to make of it.

"Who are you?" Destiny asked.

The Asiatic reacted to her question with a rush of sounds—all gibberish to me. Drawing a breath, the foreigner pointed to his eyes.

"Shiny me," he said. "Shiny me."

"Shiny what?" I asked.

"Shiny me," he repeated. In pantomime he gestured to his face and body again. "Shiny me."

I turned to Destiny. "What's he saying?"

"Sounds like 'Chinese me,'" she replied.

The man nodded as though he had heard familiar words. "Shiny me! Shiny me!"

"China?" she asked. "Chinese?"

He nodded again. "Aha!"

Destiny turned to me. "He seems friendly. Pull Boy away. Maybe he'll come down."

I stared at her. Moments ago she had been frightened out of her wits by the mere prospect of encountering someone or some creature in the cave. Now she was eager to make friends with a treed Asiatic.

I shook my head. "He's inscrutable."

"What does that mean?"

"Can't trust him."

"How do you know?"

"Mister Porter said so," I replied. "Don't you remember the Marco Polo lessons?"

"I don't care what Icky said," she replied.

"The Asiatic was spying on us," I reminded her. "When we left our camp, he rifled the packs."

"But he didn't steal anything. Maybe he was just curious. . . ."

I broke in: "Boy ran him off before he had time to rob us."

She gave that observation some thought. "I heard Pa and Loy talking about the mines. They said miners spoke every language from Asia to Europe, China to Cornwall. Pa said foreigners are taking over the whole country."

We gazed up at the treed man. He did not seem to represent much of a threat, but I figured we should give him plenty of room.

She went on: "Maybe he can tell us how to get to Revlis."

To my mind, that was one more cock-eyed notion. "He speaks two words of English . . . and I'm still not sure what they mean."

"Pull Boy away," she repeated. "If I can get that Asiatic down here, I'll scratch some lines in the dirt."

"Lines?"

"For sketches."

"Sketches," I repeated. I shook my head. "He might attack us."

She looked upward. "If this Asiatic has a knife or gun, he'd have used it by now."

I did not reply, but had to admit she made a point. I looked up. One of the man's hands was scratched and bleeding, probably from scampering up the dead tree. Destiny was right about one thing. He did not look threatening, perched up there as he was.

"Michael, take Boy away," she insisted. "Take him away." She added: "If the Asiatic tries to hurt me, sic Boy on him."

I did not think any of this was a good idea. I did not understand what she meant by "sketches." But I moved to the trunk of the tree, bent down, and grabbed Boy. He growled. This time both of my hands were free when I pulled him away from his quarry.

Boy was strong, but I managed to manhandle him, shoving and dragging him through the willows back to our campsite. Tail wagging vigorously, Boy liked our wrestling game. He licked my face, but still had to be restrained when he lunged and tried to claw his way back to his quarry. I wrapped both arms around the mastiff, and held him fast.

In the process I must have earned a measure of trust from the foreigner. When Destiny waved at him, he descended the tree and jumped to the ground. He bowed to her.

With beckoning gestures, Destiny led him

through willows to the damp bank of the beaver pond. He looked on while she found a stick and used it to inscribe lines in the mud. Still holding Boy, I raised up for a better view. Then I understood her purpose. In simple drawings, she depicted store buildings with false fronts, rectangles for doors and windows. Adding circles with short, radiating lines, she sketched spokes in wagon wheels. She finished with crude drawings of horses.

"Do you understand, Shiny Me?" she asked.

He nodded, but clearly did not comprehend the point of it all.

Destiny gestured to the west, and shrugged in a theatrical gesture. Looking all around, she held up her hands to signal bafflement. Then she spoke.

"We are lost."

Shiny Me nodded sympathetically. "Aha."

Whether it was a word, a gesture, or a certain look in her eyes, I did not know, but in those moments Shiny Me understood. I saw compassion register in his expression, and I heard it in his tone of voice. *Aha* now meant: *Yes, I know the way to the white man's village in the mountains.*

He gestured to Destiny and me, waving at us to follow him.

Boy had lost his hostility toward the stranger after he had sniffed him and decided he was no longer a mortal enemy. The man we came to call Shiny Me guided us to his camp. He lived in a cave at the base of the rock cliff. Small and nearly hidden by brush, this cave was close to the one we had entered.

Shiny Me knelt at streamside. He demonstrated his skill in panning sand scooped from the creekbed. Then he reached into a pocket and pulled out a tobacco sack. Loosening the drawstring, he inverted the small, white cotton sack and poured out a handful of gold nuggets ranging in size from buckshot to pinto beans. He smiled.

Destiny and I looked at one another. "Aha!" we said in unplanned unison, and the three of us laughed.

In that moment, I knew. Somehow, perhaps on account of our youthfulness and lack of guile, we had gained this man's trust.

Shiny Me prepared a meal for us. He gave a portion to Boy, thereby making a friend for life. At our host's direction, Destiny and I knelt around a wooden bowl and ate with our fingers. Shiny Me offered chopsticks, but we declined.

I did not know what the two sticks were, and I did not understand his urgent gestures. He meant to instruct us in their use. Dismayed, Shiny Me watched two young savages eat with their fingers. I stole glances at the foreigner as he ate in a civilized manner, a man skilled in techniques and customs dating back 5,000 years in human history.

The food was unique. Pale meat was cubed with short, sure strokes of a razor-sharp knife. The knife itself was drawn from a thin sheath under his waistband. Destiny and I exchanged a glance. He had been armed, after all. From his deft use of that knife, I knew he could have harmed us or slashed Boy's throat if that had been his intent.

Other than clumps of rice and small bowls of black tea, I did not recognize the food or the spices. It was flavorful, and, even though strange to the tongue, the food was a welcome break from our steady diet of unseasoned trout. Both Destiny and Boy ate ravenously.

I ate slowly. Destiny did not notice my gastronomic reticence, and I kept my thoughts to myself. For as we sat around that wooden bowl, I could not help but wonder if we were eating the brains of a bear.

Led by the tail-wagging, energetic dog and followed by a long-eared, long-suffering burro, Shiny Me acted as our guide. We soon learned we had missed the freight road by six or seven miles, no more. From our camp by the beaver pond, Shiny Me led us over a ridge and into the bottom of a deep cañon. That cañon opened to a meadow. Half a mile away we came upon a rutted wagon road. It followed the course of another tributary to Antelope Creek.

Shiny Me halted. In the dirt he drew his own version of store fronts, wagon wheels, and a horse. Then he pointed toward a prominent mountain range, due west, capped by snow and glaciers.

Shiny Me stepped back a pace and bowed. His message was clear.

Destiny signaled him. Having devised her own version of pantomime, she bid farewell with her hand placed over her heart. Shiny Me smiled and answered in like manner.

"Icky was wrong," she said as Shiny Me left us and walked back the way we had come.

"Wrong about what?"

"Asiatics," she replied. "Shiny Me is not inscrutable. He's friendly."

The freight road leading through deep cañons and over high peaks was little more than twin ruts worn into soil and stone. Boulders had been scarred and dirt pulverized by iron-rimmed wheels bearing heavy loads. Now with Boy bounding ahead and the burro bringing up the rear, our little caravan followed those ruts.

The climb over the first mountain was like the others—lengthy, but not steep. Switchbacks had been cut in grades to favor eight oxen or six mules in a team. Turnouts were numerous. By tradition, wagons and coaches heading uphill yielded to those coming down. Empty or loaded, backing a wagon down to a turnout was a safer maneuver than backing it up the grade.

We followed the road for two days, encountering stagecoaches and freight outfits. Chipmunks, marmots, butterflies, and small, darting birds braved afternoon showers of rain mixed with hailstones.

Unlike prairie lands, few birds of prey patrolled these skies. This terrain where stately pines had once stood bough to bough was reduced to eroded slopes of weathered pine stumps and exposed roots. Nesting places for raptorial birds were gone, the trees felled long ago by loggers and then picked clean by firewood gatherers.

At higher elevations we passed head-frames. Horizontal beams suspended pulleys and rusted cables over mine shafts. With abandoned mines and stamp mills, we saw the shells of cabins, bunkhouses, mess halls, outhouses—all of them unoccupied and unadorned. Many structures slanted southward, yielding to the push of winds. Gaping holes opened where windows and doors had once stood, and rusted stovepipes protruded at odd angles from sagging roofs, indicating the thefts of cook stoves.

Such relics in ruin bore testament to the exodus of 1893, the catastrophic aftermath of the federal government's adoption of the gold standard. In Colorado silver was king, and the reign had been long and lucrative. Owners and investors, flush one day, were bankrupt the next.

The political battle over bimetallism and the issue of free silver floating on the world markets had been joined by the finest orators of the day. William Jennings Bryan himself addressed crowds throughout Colorado and the West. He predicted our nation's "crucifixion on a cross of gold," if politicians in Washington failed to reverse the policy. Despite heroic efforts and dire predictions, with a single Presidential signature, the price of silver plummeted. Westerners suffered immediately, yet doomsday predictions of a nation in ruin never materialized.

In later years my genealogical searches for "Jennings" led to dead ends—literally, when I explored birth and marriage records, and then toured cemeteries in search of headstones. Through it all, from church congregation rosters to tax records, I was never able to link my father's branch of the Jennings family tree to the renowned WJB, the Great Commoner, the man who should have been President.

Destiny and I heard the tinkling of a bell. Delicate music emanating from the spheres? Boy heard it, too, and growled. He charged an unseen adversary. Before rounding the next bend in the road, he halted at my command.

Presently a burly teamster appeared around the bend. The shaggy man walked beside an ox-drawn ore wagon. I saw the glint of a small silver bell hanging from the neck of the lead ox. The contrast was mighty—a delicate bell hanging from the wrinkled, hairy neck of a plodding beast.

That rig was followed by five others, each one manned by a bullwhacker. Destiny grabbed the burro's rope, and we stepped aside to make room on the narrow road. Loaded with dark concentrate, the heavy vehicles crawled past us. The creep-along pace allowed the men to control the momentum of heavy loads.

The six teamsters were a foul-smelling, unkempt, shaggy lot. As they walked past, each man eyed us, some offering a single nod in greeting. Clearly we were an unexpected sight, and none of them knew what to make of us. Thick-bearded and scraggly-haired, they wore woolen trousers, flannel shirts, dirty braces, and black or brown felt hats with sweat-rimmed brims. From bandanna neckerchiefs to box-toed boots, each man was coated with the powdery dust churned by wagon wheels and stirred by hoofs. In addition to bullwhips clenched in gloved hands, revolvers were holstered, cut-down shotguns stowed in easy reach.

The first teamster shouted—"Whoa!"—and the others echoed his call. Plodding beasts whacked with whip handles halted. Brakes were set. The dark-bearded teamster first in line peered down the road behind us. He seemed to be expecting to see something down there. Baffled, he turned to us and yanked the sweat-rimmed hat off his head.

"Where's your ma?"

When neither Destiny nor I answered his barked question, he spat.

"You squirts alone?" he demanded, and spat again.

Destiny stepped back from a spray of chaw-laced spittle. "That's none of your business."

The bullwhacker stiffened. "Back talk me, sonny, and I'll swat you." To underscore his point, he advanced a step.

Boy growled, baring teeth.

"Don't hit my brother . . . !"

The bullwhacker ignored me, but with one look at the mastiff, he retreated. Eyeing Boy, his right hand drifted to the grips of his holstered revolver. "Call off your damned dog. Call him off, or I'll shoot him."

"Here, Boy. Sit."

The mastiff obeyed, sat, and looked up at me with his tail wagging. When I said—"Down."—he went down without hesitation.

The teamster spat again. "Dog's trained, huh?"

I nodded. He admired Boy, and for the moment he seemed to have forgotten his question to Destiny and me.

"Trained good, is he?"

"Yes, sir."

With the other teamsters looking on, he knelt down and cast a critical eye at Boy. "Is he scarred up?"

The question surprised me. Not knowing how to answer, I shook my head.

"What would you sell him for?"

"Boy isn't for sale."

"Hell, kid, everything's for sale."

"Not Boy."

He eyed me. "Well, if you was to part with him, what would your price be?"

I shook my head. I wished he would drop the subject.

"Not even for. . . ." His voice trailed off. "Twenty dollars?"

"No, sir."

"Twenty-five?"

I shook my head.

"Hell, kid," he said in mounting impatience, "have you ever had twenty-five dollars to your name?"

Destiny spoke up. "Leave us alone."

The bullwhacker jerked his head at her. "Stay out of this, squirt." He turned to me. "All right. Fifty. I'll give you fifty dollars for the dog . . . right here, right now."

I shook my head again.

"You sure he ain't scarred up?" the teamster demanded. He went on: "Fighting dogs get tore up sometimes. Takes the fight clean out of 'em."

"Boy's not a fighting dog," I said.

"Hell, he ain't," he said. "Maybe you don't know it, kid, but this here's a fighting breed." He spat. "Now, I'm asking one more time. What's your price on him?"

When I answered with another shake of my head, he swore mightily. A teamster standing behind him chuckled.

"Kinda sounds like he means it, Rafe."

Rafe cast a sour look at him. "Stay out of this, Saul."

114

Saul merely chuckled again.

I looked at him. Sandy-haired with his beard and mustache trimmed a bit, he asked the question Rafe had posed.

"How did you two kids end up out here, all alone?"

"Damn it, Saul, I told you. Butt out."

"I'm not bidding on the dog," Saul said. He turned to me. "Answer me, kid. How'd you end up out here in this wild country all by yourselves?"

Enacting our plan, I introduced myself as Michael, and Destiny as my brother Joe.

Looking on, the other teamsters bunched around us. One opened a can of Prince Albert and filled his pipe, tamping tobacco in the scorched bowl with his thumb. He fired it, listening intently with the others as I described our trek from a farm in Columbine County to this mountainside. I made no other mention of our background, of Noah Locke, the Quincy sisters, or Shiny Me.

On cue, Destiny put a polish on the tale when she described a raging barn fire that took our mother's life and killed our horses. We were left searching for Pa, a miner familiar with Revlis.

"Not much left of Revlis," Saul said. He thought about that and asked: "What's your pa's name?"

"Eckstrum," Destiny replied. "Bobby Eckstrum. He has a brother named Loy."

"Eckstrum, Eckstrum," repeated the bullwhacker who smoked a pipe. He shook his head and exhaled a cloud of smoke. "Ain't heard the name. You boys heard it?"

The other men shook their heads.

Saul spoke up. "Some mining men who wander these mountains leave their right names behind. They take a new name, work a few shifts, and fill their bellies in the mess hall. Then they collect their pay and go off prospecting for the mother lode."

"Or turn tail," Saul added, "whipped, and headed for home."

"Pa's not at home," Destiny said.

I saw Saul studying her.

"Most miners in Revlis," said another bull-whacker, "pulled stakes after the Crash."

"That's a fact," said another. "The smart ones are long gone. Nobody left here but us dumb shits."

Rafe rubbed his chaw-stained beard and wiped a wet hand on his trouser leg. He eyed Destiny. "You got a little bitty girly voice, squirt. How old are you?"

"None of your business," she replied.

The teamster's expression first registered surprise, then anger. "I'm warning you, squirt. Back talk will get you smacked."

I cast a quick glance at her. I knew she disliked this man, and I figured she hated being called "squirt." I caught her eye.

A shake of my head was a signal for her to keep her mouth shut. At once I saw defiance in her expression, and all the while Saul continued gazing at her. A conflict now might result in revealing her gender. I did not know what would happen then. I tried to deflect their interest in her.

"Tell us how to get to Revlis," I said, "and we'll go on our way."

Rafe cast a humorless look at me. "I'm trying to tell you for your own damned good. You squirts got no notion of what you're getting into. I'm telling you. Skedaddle back where you came from. Both of you. Skedaddle."

In a pose of defiance, Destiny placed her hands on her hips and glowered at him. To me, it was a girlish pose. I lowered my gaze, fearful of somehow revealing an obvious fact.

"Don't tell me what to do," she said.

"Damned if you ain't got a mouth on you," Rafe said.

Saul stepped between them. "He's trying to tell you kids road agents work these mountain passes like pirate raiders on the high seas."

"Road agents," I repeated.

Saul nodded. "They'll clean you plumb out. They'll take ever'thing you own . . . boots, money, burro, packs, ever'thing."

Rafe added: "And leave you for dead, likely."

Destiny asked: "Where's the sheriff?"

Rafe snorted derisively.

"The only law is handed out by miner's courts," Saul explained. "Fights are settled by fist or gun or blade."

Rafe asked suddenly: "You squirts carrying cash money?"

Destiny and I exchanged a quick look, and shook our heads.

Rafe grinned. "Lying, ain't they, Saul?"

Saul nodded. "In twelve shades of purple."

"Hell, we ain't fixing to rob you squirts," Rafe said, and spat without bothering to turn his head. "You damn' well better listen. I'm telling you. Turn back, or you're gonna get plucked cleaner than a neck-wrung chicken."

"Just as sure as hell is hot," muttered the bull-whacker puffing on his pipe. The other men solemnly nodded.

Destiny gave her answer: "We're going to Revlis."

I glanced at her. The look on her face was one I had seen before. I knew what it meant. Once her mind was made up, there was no unmaking it.

Saul said: "Lady Luck carried you kids this far. What're you going to do when she turns her back on you?"

Destiny placed her hands on her hips. "Is this the road to Revlis, or isn't it?"

Anger flashed across Saul's face, too. A long moment passed before he turned and pointed to a ridge with a white crest. "Over yonder you'll come to a fork in the road. You'll see Revlis . . . what's left of it."

The pipe-smoking bullwhacker added in a

moment of reflection: "Time was, we stopped there for beer and sausage."

"And hauled silver concentrate by the ton," Rafe said.

"Good money, regular work," said another teamster. "In those days a man could pert' near set his clock by the freight and ore outfits traveling this road."

"At fifty cents an ounce," Rafe added bitterly, "silver stays in the ground."

Saul continued: "Gold mines and crushing mills still operate in the Owl Cañon district. If your pa's a mining man, that's where he'll be, like as not." Saul offered a last piece of advice. "Don't drink water seeping out of tailings. Hear? Look for minnows and water bugs before you fill a canteen or drink from the crick. Way I figure, water that kills fish and bugs can't be healthy for two-legged critters, either."

We parted on that note. I glanced back. The teamsters stared after us, wagons and yoked oxen lined up nose to tailgate. I figured they suspected we had not confided the entire purpose of our trek to them. That was probably the subject of discussion now that we were out of earshot.

Unlike the Quincy sisters, the men had not spotted Destiny for a girl. I figured they would have, though, if we had tarried much longer. When she had placed her hands on her hips and cocked her head like she always did when expecting a fight, I saw a twelve-year-old girl standing up for herself, every feminine inch demanding respect. I figured it was only a matter of time before Saul or one of the others caught on.

"Squirt!" she said in disgust.

For myself, I was relieved to be on the road, resuming our trek.

Burro at the rear and dog in the lead, Destiny walked at my side. Without breaking stride, she looked at me and posed a question.

"Michael . . . are you . . . are you scared?"

"Some. Why?"

"All that talk . . . about road agents. . . ."

I heard her voice trail off as though she had waded into a murky sea of self-doubt. This, after standing up to burly bullwhackers and not giving them an inch.

"I feel sorry for the road agents who tangle with you," I said.

"Michael," she replied in reprimand. She paused. "Maybe we should travel at night, and hide during the day."

I lifted my hand in a sweeping gesture. Tree stumps lined bare earth like headstones. "Hide where?"

She acknowledged that point, and looked around. "What should we do?"

"Keep moving," I replied.

I glanced at her, hoping I sounded sure of myself.

Get a MOVE on came to my mind. In truth, I did not know what else to do.

We pressed on, cresting a pass over the mountain. As it turned out, we should have located a place of concealment—not from the immediate threat of outlaws, but from Zeus, ruler of the heavens in ancient Greece. We should have taken cover the moment thunder rumbled overhead.

I looked up. Black-bottomed clouds gathered like a phantom herd on the brink of a cliff. Thunder grew in volume to a menacing roar, as though unknown beasts had growled in unison. Boy tucked his tail. He held close to us. The burro walked on, unfazed. Moments later came a rainstorm riding a high wind. Those dark monsters stampeded, each cloud spawning lightning bolts as the wind swept over the summit. With every dry crackle and every bright flash, my skin tingled and my hair felt like it was standing on end.

Destiny rushed to me. We held on to one another for dear life. Leaning into wind-driven sheets of cold rain. Hailstones hit us like bullets, and water streamed off our hats. At our feet muddy rivulets flowed over pebbles and through gaps in the rocks. The miniature floods bore pieces of wildflower petals like the shards of broken gems.

Thunder boomed loud enough to dim the hearing, lightning flashes bright enough to sear the vision. When another blast lashed at us, I saw the burro stagger. From rump to shoulder, his rain-soaked body quaked. I took the lead rope in hand and led him farther down the road. We found the remains of a mine, the tunnel timbered, but partially caved in.

Destiny and I entered. We huddled under broken timbers with the wet dog. The burro planted his hoofs when I tried to pull him in. He wanted nothing to do with the dark space. The critter stayed outside, his head down as he stoically withstood the elements. Moments later the storm passed. Black clouds disappeared, and the sun came out.

We were left wet, cold, and dazed. I patted Boy on the head. I had never examined him for scars. He shook himself, shedding rain to reveal a smooth coat. I ran my hands over him, recalling Gladys's comment about a cowhand's representing Boy as a fighting dog, but in fact he was afraid of his own shadow. Just as some men do not know their own strength, I figured she did not know how fearsome she was. Boy knew better than to cross her. When he did, he got a face full of dirt.

Destiny and I eased out from the protection of the mine tunnel. Like refugees who had survived a brush with death, we looked around, assessing the damage. In the silent aftermath of violence, we beheld a scene composed of wet stumps, downed timber, and tangles of branches. One thick stump had been hit by lightning. It smoldered, and hail-stones lay on the ground around it—fire within a circle of ice. The ruination approached Biblical proportions, I figured, with vast destruction not merely from passing storms but from the hard-rock mines and stark leavings of men, too.

I heard a sharp intake of breath from Destiny. She gasped as she stepped closer to her burro. Her fingers went to a small, dark spot on a pannier buckle. I moved closer to her. The spot was a burn where lightning had struck brass. The electrical charge had bent the metal buckle, leaving a burned spot on the burro's hide the size of a half dollar.

Destiny held the rope while I removed the panniers and thick blanket. Accounts of animals struck by lightning were legion, some tales taller than others. Now we had one of our own to tell. Destiny currycombed her burro while I ran my hand over him. Except for the burn, he seemed unhurt.

We hiked down the switchbacks. The only other traffic was a coach carrying four passengers. That night we made a cold camp, and set out early in the morning. Climbing the next mountain, we descended the far side. Near the bottom, the burro suddenly bucked and sun-fished.

I hauled back on the rope, turning in the same direction to stay with him. He was strong, too strong for me to manhandle him. Braying, he fought me until he lost interest. I brought him under a measure of control before he could shed the panniers or injure himself in the effort.

At first I suspected he had been hurt, after all, and had merely reacted to pain. But when he staggered like a drunk, I wondered if the bolt of lightning had scrambled his brain. We walked on, watching him. In time he calmed. Without further resistance, he brought up the rear and assumed his regular place in the world's shortest caravan.

Descending into the cool shadows of a cañon, we were met with the sounds of a rushing creek. We came to a confluence and the fork in the road Saul had mentioned. Another half mile downslope, and the town of Revlis lay before us—or as the teamster had said: "What's left of it."

Not much was left. Warped and weathered buildings had been picked clean of usable lumber. Interior framing stood like boxy skeletons with missing bones. Doors, windows, and hardware were gone, and the structures stood in a precarious state like other plank buildings we had seen along the way.

The rope flew out of my hands when the burro reared without warning. I managed to lunge after him and grab it. Looping the rope around one wrist, I held on with both hands, and the struggle was on. This sudden move from a stoic critter surprised me. I wondered again if the lightning had scrambled his brain.

"Michael."

The burro hopped and the dog barked. I turned and followed Destiny's gaze. A gaunt man in frontier garb emerged from the shadows of a dilapidated building. I recognized his gimpy stride as he led a long-legged black mule. The burro's brain had not been scrambled, after all. It was the presence of his arch-enemy, not a lightning strike, that had set him off.

I glanced at Destiny. Jaw set, she faced the old-timer dressed in dirty buckskins, moccasins, and a hat with a rattlesnake skin for a band.

"How did you find us?" Destiny demanded.

Noah Locke shrugged off her question. "Warn't much of a chore."

Chapter Six

"What do you want?" Destiny demanded.

"Don't much matter what I'm a-wantin'," Mr. Locke answered. "It's what Hale's a-wantin' that counts."

"What does the sheriff want?" Destiny asked.

"You two runaways brung in, for starters," he said. "He's got a raft of questions for you."

"What questions?"

"That's up to him to tell you, now, ain't it?"

Destiny eyed him, her anger seething. It was that look I had seen before, a look that could drive a railroad spike into a man's forehead. "Mister Locke, you're not taking us anywhere."

"We'll just see about that," he said.

She insisted: "I am not going back to Columbia."

Emboldened by her words, I said: "Me, neither."

"Reckon you will," he said.

Destiny shook her head.

"You will," Mr. Locke said, "iffen I have to drag you there myself. Don't think I don't know what's going through your danged heads. You won't get away with sneaking up on my weak side this time."

Hands propped on her hips, Destiny mocked him: "We'll just see about that."

Mr. Locke scowled. If he had expected two twelve-year-olds to knuckle under to threats, he was mistaken. It was a lesson he should have learned by now.

"How did you find us?" Destiny asked suddenly. "You couldn't have tracked us all this way." She thought a moment. "Unless Gladys Quincy put you on our trail."

"Quincy who?" Mr. Locke asked.

I answered his question. "The Quincy sisters run cattle under the Lazy Three brand."

"Never heard of 'em," he said with a glance at me. "Nor that 'ere brand, neither."

Destiny asked: "Then how did you find us?"

"Like anybody else would," he replied. "I cut north outen Columbia County and follered the freight and coach road due west, due west into these-here danged mountains." He rubbed his back-side, grimacing. "Too many days in the saddle. Piles, don't you know."

"No, I don't know," Destiny said, "and I don't want to, either."

"Reckon there's something we can see eye-to-eye

on, you and me," he said. He rubbed himself again. "My poor old ass end."

Destiny turned away in disgust.

Mr. Locke gestured to the mastiff. "Where'd you find that 'ere big dog?"

"He found us," I said.

Mr. Locke pushed his weathered hat up on his forehead and regarded us. "That makes all of you runaways, then, don't it?" He turned to me. "How in hell did you land here?"

"We followed Antelope Creek," I said.

"All this way?" he asked, amazed. "You follered that 'ere crick all the way from Columbia to this 'ere spot where we're standing?"

I nodded.

A smile crept over his leathery face. "Same as trappers going after beaver in the old days, afoot in the old ways." He paused as he calculated our trek. "You never angled north to the main road a-tall then, did you? That's how I got plumb ahead of you without crossing your trail."

Destiny and I exchanged a quick look. Our ignorance of east-west roadways had led us on an overland course. A route that had looked easy on the school's wall map was in truth the most difficult route to Revlis imaginable.

"Somebody must have told you where to look for us," Destiny insisted. "Who?"

"I done told you," he replied. "Hale."

"How did the sheriff know?" she asked.

"Hale says you made a wild claim," he replied. "It plumb gave you away."

Destiny was baffled. "What claim?"

"The man I shot out of the saddle might not have been your pa a-tall," he replied. "You claimed it could have been Bobby's brother, a gent by the name of Loy. Loy Eckstrum. Ain't that right?"

Destiny conceded that point with a single nod.

Mr. Locke went on: "Hale says when Bobby got hisself a snoot full, he'd brag up a storm. He done bragged about him and Loy high-grading ore out of the Dollar Be Mine. Other mines, too. Old habits die hard, I reckon."

"Old habits," Destiny repeated. "What do you mean?"

"Them sacks of concentrate behind your shack," he explained. "Me and Hale, we found them under some brush."

"I don't know what you're talking about," Destiny said.

"Don't lie to me," Locke said.

"You mean . . . you mean those bags of black sand?" Destiny asked.

Mr. Locke showed missing teeth when he grinned. "That ain't sand."

"What is it?"

"Hale took samples," he replied. "Assayer's report came back at eighty-nine percent silver."

Destiny thought about that. "But silver isn't worth much, is it?"

"Depends," he said.

"On what?" she asked.

"On what a feller paid for it," Mr. Locke said. "Iffen a feller never paid nothing for it, then it's one hunnert percent profit, ain't it?"

Destiny gazed at the panniers as though looking into the past. "All I know is, Loy brought those sacks on the back of a burro. He told me it was black sand, and to stay away from it."

"Reckon he lied to you," Mr. Locke said. He waved his arm to encompass the town site. "So, here I sits, a-waitin' for you two to get here. I was starting to wonder iffen Hale had this thing figured wrong, or iffen you two was dead or bad hurt. Then I seen you. Seen you coming down them switchbacks. Seen you from a long way off, among them old stumps." He laughed. "Seen that burro get prancy on you, too. You danged near lost him, didn't you?"

Destiny studied the ground at her feet. I figured I knew what was going through her mind. Until this moment, she had believed the lawman in Columbia had not heeded her words when she had confronted him after the burial. Sheriff Hale must have thought better of it later, probably after Locke had returned to town with news of the runaways he had encountered on the bank of Antelope Creek. When Sheriff Hale and Mr. Locke put two and two together, they must have come up with murder and a stolen payroll. The bagged silver concentrate pointed to Revlis.

Mr. Locke went on: "Maybe your Uncle Loy is the one who killed Mister Simms, and maybe he ain't. Loy or Bobby, either one, could be holed up hereabouts with the Bar-S payroll. . . ."

"Pa din't steal it!" Destiny interrupted. "He never killed anyone, either."

"How do you know that for fact?" Mr. Locke asked.

Jaw clenched, she replied: "I just know."

"Iffen it warn't him, then who done it?"

"Go away, Mister Locke," she said. "Go away and leave us alone."

"Iffen you was as big as that mouth of yourn," he said, "you might could order me around. But you ain't big. You ain't big a-tall."

I saw Destiny's face flush as she stared at him in quiet anger.

Mr. Locke paused, and finally spoke in a tone that was conciliatory. "Truth is, Destiny, this thing don't sit right."

"What do you mean?"

"I done lost sleep over it."

Her anger peaking, I saw a certain indefinable look cross her face. I figured this was the first time Noah Locke had called her by name—to her face, anyway—and the note of compassion in his voice had an impact on her. She still gazed at him. I figured she was trying to read the truth writ in the lines of a weathered face.

"Over what?" she asked.

"Lining up my gun sights that day," he replied, "and squeezing the danged trigger."

I pushed my eyeglasses up on my nose and watched him drag gnarled fingers through his white mustache. "Like I done told you, I didn't know who it was in my sights. All I knowed was, the rider was going hell-for-leather, and the horse stoled from Mister Simms's corral warn't shod. Sure as hell, I never figured I could hit a man at that range, much less take half his danged head off."

Destiny winced.

"I can't make it right with you," he went on. "I know that. But maybe I can lend a hand."

"How?"

"Columbia County posted a ree-ward of two thousand dollars."

"Two thousand dollars," Destiny repeated. "For what?"

"For bringing in the man who done robbed and kilt Mister Roger Simms," he replied. He paused for dramatic effect. "I figured you'd be inner-rested."

Destiny repeated that word as though she had never heard it before. "Interested."

"What I said," Mr. Locke said. "Bobby or Loy, either one. Tell me where he is, and I'll bring him in. Then we'll split that 'ere ree-ward, you and me, as soon as Hale hands it over."

I watched as she stared at him.

"Right down the middle," he went on. "Thousand for you, thousand for me."

"Mister Locke, I don't know where my pa is, or Uncle Loy, either. Even if I did, I wouldn't collect a reward."

"I figured you might balk at the notion of turning your kin over to the law," he said. "You oughter think it over, though. Somebody's gonna get that money. Might as well be you."

When she offered no opinion, he added: "I figured all along you know more about your pa than you ever told Hale. That's the truth, ain't it? You can tell me. . . ."

"No!" Destiny said, her voice rising. "No!"

Driven back a pace by her outburst, he turned to me. "What about you?"

"Huh?"

"What has she done told you about her pa?" Locke asked. "Or Loy, either?"

Destiny protested until he cut her off.

"I'm asking this 'ere Jennings boy, not you," Mr. Locke said.

Picking up on the threat, Boy bared his teeth and growled. Mr. Locke warily eyed the mastiff until I called him. Tail wagging, Boy came to me and sat at my feet.

"What has she done told you about her kin?" the old-timer asked again.

I shook my head. "Nothing."

I saw enough skepticism in his eyes to know he disbelieved me. But it was true. In all of our travels and travails, Destiny and I had never discussed her father. Or mine, either, not after that first day when she had asked about my punishment—and promptly fell asleep while I answered.

Mr. Locke said: "Think on it, son."

"On what?"

"Gettin' your fair share of the ree-ward," he replied irritably, as though I had not been paying attention. "A thousand dollars is yourn as soon as Hale hands it over. Think what you could do with a thousand dollars. Buy yourself the finest saddle horse outen the Columbia livery barn . . . new saddle and gear . . . new deer rifle . . . new hat . . . all the danged duds you ever wanted at Knowles's mercantile." He repeated: "One thousand dollars. Chew on that notion, and see how it tastes." I saw his bushy eyebrows arch when he added conspiratorially: "Maybe more money, iffen you get my drift."

I did not get his drift, or anything close to it. I knew he was trying to bribe me with fanciful promises, and I knew he was doing a poor job of concealing his motives. Most of all, I knew he was on the wrong trail. I had no information to impart, no secrets to reveal.

Destiny got his drift. I heard an anguished sound from her, an utterance of disgust beyond the spoken word.

"It's not the reward, is it?" she demanded. "It's the payroll. You're after the Bar-S payroll, and you still think I know where it is. That's the truth, isn't it?"

Mr. Locke's wrinkled face could have been chis-

133

eled from stone. I turned to Destiny. I figured she regarded his lack of a quick denial as an admission of guilt.

"Hell, you youngsters are full of spit and vinegar," he said, "and you figure you're always gonna be. Well, you ain't. Take my word on that. Someday you'll run out of steam. Then you'll be up against it. Just like I am . . . sore ass, and all."

Uncertain of his meaning, Destiny and I looked at one another.

"Getting too old to work," he went on, "and too stove up to sleep on hard ground under a pile of flea-bit hides. Can't run a trap line no more, either. Even iffen I could, beaver pelts and wolf hides don't bring much."

I watched as he drew a labored breath. "But damned iffen I'll live out my days scratching dirt at the county poor farm or gathering eggs in the charity hen house, neither. . . ." His voice trailed off, and he paused before he spoke again. "Supposing, just supposing, a feller was to come across that 'ere payroll. Just supposing. How would he know? Get my drift? Cash is cash. Nobody knows perzactly where cash comes from. Nobody knows who carried it before you got it. I figure most folks have carried cash that was stoled, some-time or other." As though citing a philosophical conundrum for the ages, Mr. Locke posed his question: "How's a fellar to know?"

Destiny knew. "If it comes out of a Bar-S saddlebag, or the pocket of a man who was in the ranch house, then you know who it belongs to."

Locke shook his head. "That's just it, see? That 'ere money was stoled, pure and simple. The gent it was stoled from is dead. He ain't got no use for it no more. Now it belongs to whoever gets a-holt of it. That's the danged truth."

I pushed my eyeglasses up on the bridge of my nose and peered at him. For once in my life, I weighed moral values and considered the implications of action and reaction. With the old-timer eyeing us like some autodidact reeking of self-importance, I wondered what Mr. Porter would say. Then, as though Ichabod's voice drifted through the spheres from Columbia to Revlis, the whole issue came into focus for me.

"Stolen."

Mr. Locke turned to me. "Huh?"

"Stolen money belongs to whoever earned it," I said in a halting voice. "Some of it . . . belongs to the Bar-S ranch hands who get paid every month . . . the rest belongs to somebody who inherits the ranch."

Mr. Locke had little patience for my line of reasoning. He dismissed my opinion with a wave of his gnarled hand, and turned to Destiny.

"Put me on the trail of Bobby or Loy, either one," he said. "What the hell. Maybe you can prove they're innocent. Have you thought of that?"

When Destiny did not reply, Mr. Locke made a

magnanimous offer. "I reckon Hale don't need to know perzactly where you two run off to. We'll keep it between us. What do you say?"

"I don't care what that lawman knows," she said. "I'm not going back to Columbia."

Mr. Locke gazed at her in silence.

"Don't follow us any more, either," she added.

I watched as they stared at one another in mounting hostility, neither one showing any quit. Mr. Locke squinted as though staring into the sun.

"I range where I please," he said. "Anywhere a-tall."

"Mister Locke," Destiny said, "put your sore ass in a sling and range somewhere else."

Angered, Noah Locke swore under his breath. Instead of battling, his shoulders sagged. He'd had his fill of us. Turning to his mule, he snugged the cinch, and grasped the saddle horn.

I saw him grimace and heard him groan as he brought his leg up and thrust his foot into the stirrup. In a series of stiff-legged hops, he grunted and hauled himself into the saddle with great exertion. Once aboard, he took up the reins.

We watched him ride away, just as we had watched him that day on the bank of Antelope Creek when he had caught up with us. He did not have a high regard for us then, either.

Leading the burro, Destiny and I walked the rutted, weed-grown streets of Revlis. A few residences

136

with curtained windows and trimmed yards were obviously occupied. We did not attempt a thorough search of the town site or question any residents. We figured Noah Locke had done that for us.

We passed a schoolhouse where whitewash peeled from the few remaining boards still standing. The bell tower was empty. Vacant squares and rectangles were all that was left of doors and casement windows. Destiny and I walked around the playground. Two swing sets and a teeter-totter stood rusting and forlorn like dark skeletons. Few places on earth are as haunting as an empty school playground, and an eerie sensation crept over me.

I thought about a once-bustling mining town with a busy school, a place countless men, women, and children had called home. Now, with no shouts from boys or shrieks from girls, a strange sensation came over me. Like a cold wind on a hot day, the source could have been ethereal beings roaming just beyond the range of human vision, their voices muted by the wind.

Fanciful, I know, but on that day in that place, I could not deny the sensation of the past somehow still alive in the present.

I was further spooked when Boy growled at unseen enemies. Hair stood up on the back of his neck. In the next instant Destiny grasped my arm. A mangy, feral dog slunk out of shadows cast by a tumble-down structure. He was followed by other mongrels, a pack, each mutt growling and snarling, their predator eyes fixed on Boy.

We halted. I counted eleven dogs. They advanced, growling as they slowly encircled us. Ribs showing under hides as mangy and dirty as starving wolves, they challenged a new dog invading their domain. The pack leader crouched, snarled, and inched closer. Wolf-like, his pedigree could well have been half coyote and half the neighbor's. He snarled and bluffed a charge. Other dogs yelped as though cheering him on.

Boy moved to the middle of the street with deliberation, like a boxer taking the ring. He looked back at me, and halted. The maneuver seemed like one part of a drill, a training sequence, perhaps from the cowhand who had sold Boy to the Quincy sisters. Whether it was or not, a fight was imminent. By instinct or by training, Boy waited for the battle to come to him.

Destiny whispered to me urgently. "Michael . . . call him."

I shook my head. "Too late."

If I gave Boy a command now, he would turn his back on a pack of mongrels primed for attack. Watching the leader, I figured the fight was between him and Boy, and I wanted to keep it that way.

Boy growled again. He stood among the weeds in the street, front legs slightly spread, buttock muscles bunched. There was no bluff in him. When the pack leader came within range, Boy charged.

The fight was as brief as it was sudden. Boy sent the pack leader rolling in the dirt and into tall weeds, pursued him, and bit him. The pack leader howled in pain. Boy sank his teeth into his upper shoulder, lifted him off his feet, and dropped him. Scrambling away, the mutt yelped and howled in pain or fear—or equal parts of both. The others followed at a dead run.

"Boy. Here, Boy."

The mastiff shook himself. He did not pursue the town dog. In answer to my call, he turned and trotted back to Destiny and me, tail wagging, pink tongue out. He sat at my feet and gazed up at us. I petted his big head while Destiny rubbed his upper shoulders. In the next moment a woman's voice carried to us.

"Watch out for them dogs! They're mean! Mean as Satan!"

Destiny and I turned toward the shrill voice. We walked past the shell of a livery barn to a sway-backed log cabin. A stout woman was hanging wet clothes on a line. She wore an apron over a long, pale green dress. A pioneer-style sunbonnet shaded her eyes when she looked at us.

I waited with the burro and Boy while Destiny walked down the slope and spoke to her. Presently she came back.

"That lady said a stinking trapper camped here."

"Mister Locke?"

She nodded. "He was asking for a miner named

Eckstrum. She hasn't seen him." Destiny paused. "She says folks in Revlis are die-hards. They hang on because they think silver will be king again."

Chapter Seven

In no small measure I credit my span of life to timely advice from the bullwhacker known to me only as Saul. He cautioned Destiny and me against drinking clouded water that seeped from mine tailings, or consuming clear water from any creek or pond devoid of aquatic life.

Misinformed travelers of the era consumed these waters, believing them to be an elixir. Named as remedies from the bowels of the earth, the waters were said to be a cure-all. Entrepreneurs bottled the stuff, selling it to flatlanders under the label of *The Great Mountain Fountain of Youth & Good Health*. I have often wondered how many imbibers died young.

Saul's advice was sound. Modern science has since proven water bearing acid waste is not medicinal. It was poisonous then, and still is.

For the next three days Destiny and I trudged along the wagon road beside the rushing creek. Water cascaded over rocks and around boulders in a dull roar. We made room for stagecoaches, coming and going, high-wheeled vehicles bearing luggage atop and dust-coated passengers within.

The big coaches teetered at every turn as the drivers handled the reins with both hands while shouting at their teams. Freight and ore wagons also wended their way through the cañon between two mountains. Bullwhackers eyed us, but, unlike Rafe, none stopped to question our presence in the high country.

The creek was ice cold. Clear and inviting, headwaters emanated from snow-covered glaciers snagged in the highest reaches of the mountains. I knelt beside the creek while Destiny tended Boy and the burro. Riffles held no trout, and pools were devoid of darting minnows and skittering bugs.

We drank from our canteens. Farther on, we refilled them from a dripping snow bank. At a higher altitude, Boy and the burro drank their fill from ponds where minnows dodged our shadows, and mosquitoes with a thirst for blood came after us.

As I learned from later research, water seeping out of mine tailings was often clouded by "sediments in suspension," in the parlance of mineralogists. The process of shipping some 600,000 troy ounces of gold over a period of years had left tons of waste rock behind. This waste contained pyrite, a mineral that released sulphuric acid when exposed to water and air. Such acid drainage from the mines dissolved metals—zinc, lead, copper—known now to be harmful to humans.

Miners inhaling rock dust and dodging cave-ins

for nine-hour shifts six days a week earned a daily wage of $3. Single jacking holes by candlelight and blasting tunnels to be timbered was dangerous work. Miners' lives were lost while owners and investors were enriched. Plump gents in their finery resided in the great mansions of San Francisco, Chicago, New York City where squads of servants were paid twice as much as the men who blasted solid rock and hauled ore out of long tunnels or lifted it out of deep, dark shafts.

The irony of owners and investors acquiring vast wealth while hard-rock miners lived in poverty and worked in daily danger was well documented. Such bald inequities paved the way later for strikes and the organization of labor unions. Not so well known was the toll taken by rock dust clogging a man's lungs and acid waste eating his gut. Whether gold was destined for ladies' jewelry or silver for a gent's watch chain, the byproducts were the same—dense dust and deadly acid.

Had he known of it, I figured Mr. Porter would have speared this paradox as a means of exposing his students to the cruel facts of life and death among miners from the Rockies to the Sierras. Paradox, indeed. In his lectures, Icky often cited Latin and Greek sources. Paradox is derived from the Greek *paradoxos*, meaning "in conflict with expectations." Given the tremendous wealth extracted from the mines, one would expect miners to live in comfort if not the vast luxury of moneyed men waddling about in their mansions.

Not that Icky would have stopped there. I figured he would concoct a mathematical equation to demonstrate the proportion of acid waste to material assets. "The greater the poison, the richer the man" could well have been another of his obscure adages. Given his philosophical turn of mind, would he equate orchestral music with the tinkling of a silver bell hanging from the hairy, wrinkled neck of an ox? Or would a diamond-clear mountain brook laced with acid capture his wit?

My thoughts wandered over this imaginary terrain until Destiny and I rounded a bend and came upon a herd of deer. She smiled and pointed at twelve or fifteen does and young males, all of them standing as still as statuary. They observed us from the edge of a pine forest. Only when one of them moved did the others turn and gracefully bound into the trees. Another mile or so farther, we rounded a bend and spooked a herd of elk. The bulls raised their heads, looked at us, and wheeled. Tipping their antlers back, they ran into the trees and crashed through thick boughs, cows following.

We hiked past a battered buckboard wagon with tailgate boards missing. Tongue down, the vehicle was half hidden in a stand of aspens. In the gathering dusk, I saw two sway-backed horses and three men over there. With the scent of wood smoke in the air, I figured they were travelers who had found a campsite. The roadside was marked by stone-ringed fire pits and rusted tins, and we moved on until we found a level stretch of terrain beyond the trees. After scouting the immediate area, we camped in a meadow that offered a measure of privacy from the wagon road half a mile away. At nightfall Destiny and I slept under the blanket with Boy lying between us. For a time the mastiff was agitated, but I managed to calm him.

In the morning I was awakened by Destiny. She shivered. I got up and built a fire. With the blanket draped over us, we moved as close to the crackling flames as we dared while the sun came up and slowly warmed the air.

Since leaving Revlis, we had climbed in elevation. Even though higher altitudes brought us closer to the sun, each day was colder than the last. Destiny no longer wore her thin dress when we camped. She settled for the gaudy orange and maroon scarf knotted around her neck while donning her boy outfit for warmth.

Other than school topics, we had rarely spoken of the past. I had wondered about her life before we met, but did not ask. For one thing, we were both preoccupied with the present, survival being our daily concern. For another, given the notorious reputation of her father, I had sensed Destiny did not want to talk about the past.

In truth, neither did I. I did not know what the future held, but I knew it was out there in front of me somewhere, and I was more interested in what I would find beyond the next bend in the road than in reviewing past events. For those reasons, then, I was surprised on that dawning day when Destiny leaned against me under the blanket and asked about my family and life on the farm.

"You once told me. . . ." Her voice trailed off.

"Told you what?" I asked.

"About your pa."

"What about him?"

"You said . . . you said he handed you a whipping."

Perhaps Noah Locke's hammering questions had opened the door to the past. Or perhaps curiosity simply got the best of her. For whatever reason, while we shivered and gazed at leaping flames that morning, I told her about my life on the farm. Rather than speak of the tanning, I began with an account of my chores.

Destiny interrupted. As usual, she went straight to the heart of matters. First, she asked about my mother. What was she like? Was I like her? Or was I more like my father? What about my sisters? Who did they take after?

Formulating answers to her rapid-fire questions, I found this to be a difficult exercise. Time is an opaque lens. I was aware memories of my mother and sisters were fading from my mind. When I shut my eyes and visualized their faces, I drew from memories of their last day on the farm. They had changed in three years, of course, and in idle moments I wondered how they looked and acted now.

Destiny pressed me with more questions. Had Mother and I corresponded? Why not? Had I written to her? Why not? Had Father told me where they were living in Chicago? Why not?

Long ago when I had raised such questions, Father insisted Mother had departed without leaving an address where she could be reached. All we could do was wait for her letters. None came, and at the time I wondered if that was true. But, as I told Destiny, I did not confront Father. The reasons were ill formed in my mind. Partly it was out of fear of him. Another part of the equation was the lack of maturity required to put all of the pieces of the Jennings family puzzle together. I was occupied with farm chores by daylight and schoolwork by lamplight. More than I wanted to admit, I emulated my father. To him, one day's labors merely led to the next. *Work hard every day* could have been his motto. That, and *Get a MOVE on!* As a result of such harangues, I worked hard, studied diligently, and did not question him.

Thus, without my intention, the clarity of hindsight revealed a certain ambivalence toward both parents. Instinctively I wanted to emulate my father, yet at once I despised him. I missed my mother, but imitated my father's taciturn demeanor by never speaking about her. Those conflicted feelings stirred anger, leaving me with a residue of ill will.

I know that to be true now. Gazing at Destiny in the early morning chill of that mountain meadow, I confessed to her my shock upon overhearing three whispered words from those ladies in the mercantile. In my mind, their voices made an endless refrain.

She left him. She left him. She left him.

And me.

Unless Mother traveled to Colorado, I would not see her until I was old enough to travel on my own. Even then I did not know how I would ever accumulate enough money for the journey by coach to Denver and by rail to Chicago.

I did not possess a dime. I had never carried coins of my own. Other than one stick of peppermint candy from the store every other Saturday, Father never paid me. He told me I had no need for money, and, in fact, many of our transactions were bartered. For his part, Father provided shelter, clothing, eyeglasses, food—the latter usually consisting of a tin plate heaped with sow-belly and scrambled eggs—and all of the clabbered milk I could choke down. Fresh milk was either separated for cream, churned for butter, or buttermilk crocked to be sold in town. There was no room for complaint on the Jennings place. Soured milk had been good enough for Father in his childhood, and it was good enough for me in mine.

In addition to my cycle of chores, I pursued and caught runaway livestock, filled water troughs, and secured fences as needed. I gathered eggs, milked, fed animals—keeping up with all of the farmhand tasks required of me. All this without a few coins jingling in my pocket like most boys had.

Perhaps Father reasoned I stood to inherit a good farm someday, and eventual ownership of the Jennings place was ample reward for a lifetime of hard work in all seasons of the year. If such a notion guided his thinking, though, he never hinted of it to me. For all I knew, he planned to dig up the farm and take it with him when he died.

Boy whined. I fed him jerky out of my hand while Destiny looked on. In talking to her about the past, I had not intended to portray myself in a self-serving manner or convince her of my righteousness. Even at twelve I sensed Father lived as he had lived in his youth, and knew of no other way.

Destiny pressed against me in a tender gesture. She said she had wondered about me, and now she knew. Taken altogether, my decision to leave the farm had not been a last-minute leap into the unknown, after all. It had been a long time coming, a decision that coalesced after she had revealed her plan to me.

The sun warmed us while Destiny revealed pieces of her life. She had been raised in orphanages and a series of foster homes. Countless nights she had lain awake in a strange bed. In a dormitory room of the Sarah Harmon Home For Girls, she had breathed deeply with her mouth stretched open as a means of silencing her sobs. She thought about the girls who had departed, the youngsters selected by adoptive parents, and she agonized over reasons to explain why she had not been chosen.

She peered into mirrors in search of flaws. Was she hateful? Ugly? Unsmiling? Odorous? Did she possess an evil eye? Had someone lied about her? Had she been accused of a crime too horrible to name?

Such questions tormented her and, in time, brought her to a single conclusion: her file contained damning information. What it was, she could not fathom. But there could be no other answer. Prospective parents were turned away by an accusation lodged in her file. What other explanation could there be for being shunned?

Destiny was keen to read those documents. She requested them. The director, Mr. Harold Winslow, was a man who issued directives in a soft-spoken manner, a kindly voice masking inflexible adherence to iron-clad policies. The day Destiny entered his office, she trembled in fear of the man. Mr. Winslow abruptly denied her request by cutting her off in midsentence. Only strangers—those prospective parents—were allowed to peruse private files and read graphic accounts of beatings, abandonment, illegitimacy, murder, incest, rape.

The irony of it was apparent to Destiny, and she said as much to Mr. Harold Winslow. She steadied her shaking voice and offered a compromise: could someone on his staff merely describe the information contained in her file?

Request denied.

Over the years Destiny had created imaginary parents, a devoted couple she described in detail to anyone who would listen. The description rang true—to her, anyway. Mr. and Mrs. Eckstrum had been forced by circumstances to relinquish their favorite daughter. They were impoverished after her father's livery barn burned to the ground. Destiny described in excruciating detail the agonized cries of horses burning to death. In the aftermath, with one less mouth to feed in a teeming family, the other Eckstrum children could survive, barely. Destiny was strong and capable, and that was why she had been chosen to leave the family temporarily. When times were better, her mother and father would send for her.

At once Destiny knew it was all pretense. The details were lies, and she figured the girls who listened knew it. Most of them had spun yarns of their own, fanciful accounts of the reasons they lived in this place and how long they would have to stay. They all wanted to believe, and to be believed.

Like ice applied to a bruise, the lies numbed pain. And like the other girls, Destiny clung to numbing fabrications. She nurtured them as though she could breathe life into fantasy.

The truth was revealed by an errant set of keys. On a Sunday afternoon she scooped up the custodian's key ring. It was in the furnace room where she had been assigned to sweep up fine, black dust and fill bins by shoveling coal down the chute. Seizing the opportunity, she dropped the push broom and rushed through empty hallways. She stopped at the locked door of Winslow's office. In her nervously shaking hand, the fourth key opened it. Entering, she rushed to the bank of file cabinets along one wall, and opened the drawer marked E-F. She needed only seconds to find her surname, pull the file, and read it.

Eckstrum, Destiny Jane, DOB Unknown
  Mother: Name unknown. Deceased by suicide, 189?
  Father: Robert Paul Eckstrum. Inmate, State Penitentiary, Canon City, Colorado. DOB Unknown.

Terse as it was, Destiny at last knew the truth, or a part of it. Just as eye and hair color were passed through generations, so were the traits of criminals—insanity, suicide, violent behavior. No one would knowingly adopt a child sired in the union of a criminal and a woman dead by her own hand.

Destiny wrote a brief letter to Robert Paul

Eckstrum. She convinced the custodian to post her missive to Canon City by promising never to mention the careless placement of the keys that had given her access to the files.

Destiny waited for a reply, not knowing what to expect. Over six long days, nothing happened. On the seventh, she was summoned to Winslow's office.

On the director's desk lay a battered envelope. Returned from the state prison, it had obviously been opened and resealed. REJECTED/RETURNED was stamped in bold black letters on the face of it. Aware of Winslow's stare, her tears welled as she acknowledged the handwriting was hers. She mumbled a halting statement to the effect that those two words REJECTED/RETURNED summed up her life to date.

She was met by silence from the small man seated behind his half-acre desk. For once the director had no policy to cite, no glib rejoinder to shore up institutional policies as the guiding force in his decisions.

When questioned, Destiny confessed to reading the Eckstrum file, but kept the key ring secret. To no avail. Winslow merely checked the duty roster for that Sunday, and reached the logical conclusion. First, he fired the custodian. Second, he confined Destiny to a windowless room in the basement for punishment.

Punishment? In truth, she welcomed solitude.

Sobbing, she wept in the locked room until her tears were gone. The next day she was allowed to return to her bunk. In the meantime, Winslow surprised every member of his staff when he ventured outside the rules and personally contacted the prison warden. He conveyed a message by telegraph, and in two days a reply to Destiny's letter was hand-delivered from Canon City. The scrawled text was barely legible.

Reckon I am yor pa alrite. Gitten parold in 2 weeks. So the basturds say.

Bobby.

PS. Wood lak to see you sum day.

Destiny had never received a letter before. Now as she stood in the director's office, she read and reread this one in an effort to extract great meaning from few words. She wanted to know if this meant her father was coming for her, and at once she was afraid to ask.

She later found out Bobby had been paroled early by agreeing to write the letter in his own hand. He was issued new duds from head to toe. A crisp ten-dollar bill, folded once, was placed in a jacket pocket. The warden promised another ten awaited him at the Sarah Harmon Home For Girls in Denver. All he had to do to claim the money was to show up and speak to Mr. Winslow about Destiny.

Instead of spending money on the luxury of

coach fare, Bobby flagged down a farm wagon *en route* from Canon City to Pueblo. There, in the train yards, he dodged bulls armed with weighted saps or nightsticks, and hopped a northbound. He traveled to Denver with fresh air wafting in his face, a breeze tinged with a bouquet of desert sage and coal smoke from the steam engine. He breathed deeply as he took in the unobstructed view through the open door of the boxcar. Freedom had never smelled better.

Destiny met her father in the conference room of the Sarah Harmon Home For Girls. For a quarter of a century within these four walls prospective parents met and interrogated girls up for adoption. Tears of joy and sorrow had been shed here. Austere, the room possessed the stark aura of a shrine.

Now with the director and three staff members looking on, Destiny stared at her pa. Unshaven and unkempt, Bobby Eckstrum hemmed and hawed in response to questions from the staff. All the while Destiny searched for familiarity in a strange face and listened for a note of recognition in his low, halting voice. She found neither.

Offering few details about his background, Bobby answered with shrugs and a mumbled uh-huh or huh-uh. He readily admitted guilt. His part in saloon robberies—four that he confessed to—had landed him in prison. As to Destiny's mother, she was a woman he had not known well "before she died." He claimed to know nothing of her background, not even the location of the cemetery where she was interred. And, no, he did not wish to have Destiny removed from this institution, to be commended to his care.

"Ah cain't look after her none," he said. "Ah dunno what ah'll do to pull ends together for mah ownself. She's a sight better off with you folks, damned if she ain't."

Avoiding Destiny's gaze, he turned his attention to Winslow. "Got something for me?"

The director glowered. "Is that all you have to say, Mister Eckstrum?"

"Hell, yes," Bobby said. He thrust his hand out, beggar-style.

Winslow paused again, eyeing a man he clearly disliked. "Sir, she needs some help," he said quietly.

Bobby eyed him, but made no reply. His hand was still out.

With a pained look of deliberation, Winslow pulled open the lapel of his jacket and reached to an inside pocket. He drew out a ten-dollar bill, held it for a moment, and pushed it across the table.

Rattler quick, Bobby snatched it up. He shoved his chair back and stood. Smirking, he pocketed the ten as he crossed the conference room to the door. He was reaching for the handle when Destiny intercepted him.

Startled, Bobby recoiled, his outstretched hand

suspended in mid-air. For the first time their eyes met and held. Blinking, he slowly lowered his hand.

Destiny neither wept nor pleaded. Raising up on her toes, she grasped Bobby's sleeve and whispered in his ear. No one else heard the promise from her lips. Only Bobby heard her vow never to complain, never to be a hindrance. She merely wanted to be with him until she was old enough to live on her own.

Bobby pulled away. Head bowed, he opened the door and lunged into the hallway as though escaping a terrible fate.

Still, Destiny shed no tears. From the doorway, she watched her father stride down the hall toward the main entrance. He rounded the corner. Moments later the metal clad door slammed shut, the sound reverberating through the hallway like a shot.

Leaning back against the doorjamb, Destiny closed her eyes.

As she told me that morning in the mountain meadow, she had seen something in Bobby's expression, the barest hint of familial recognition. Wishful thinking or not, she held the image in her mind. That night when she lay in bed, eyes open in darkness, she merely waited for daybreak. In the morning she packed her clothing and everything she owned in a pillow slip. Seated on her bunk, then, she waited. Hours dragged. Doubts crowded her mind, and she wiped away tears. Then at midday she was summoned by a member of Winslow's staff.

Destiny came on the run, pillow slip in hand. She passed the conference room doorway and drew up as Bobby lurched out of the director's office. Destiny saw him stagger into the hall. Catching his balance, he made a game effort at squaring his shoulders. He swayed and nearly fell again. Destiny grasped his arm at the elbow and steadied him.

"Pa."

With every shred of dignity lost, his watery-eyed gaze shifted and settled on her. He scowled, but did not pull away. A long moment passed between them before he spoke.

"Awright. Hell. Come on."

Hearing those words, Winslow stepped out of his office. Three staff members followed. Halting, none of them spoke, much less intervened. They may well have been eager to be rid of Destiny Jane Eckstrum, not from any measure of ill will or even raw expediency on their part, but in recognition of the fact that in all likelihood she would reside here until the day of her eighteenth birthday.

That alone was a cruel fate. A way station, the Sarah Harmon Home merely housed girls. It was a place where abandoned girls were safe, sheltered from man and the elements, as they say. None was schooled, trained in domestic arts or manners, or prepared in any way for life beyond the front gate. At eighteen, they were merely turned out. Forced to survive in an environment as foreign as the cratered landscape of the moon, Winslow and his staff had few illusions of what the future held for Destiny Jane, for a girl like her.

In Denver, Bobby's money was soon exhausted—poured down the whiskey drain, as the saloon saw goes. He earned money for cheap rye and cold food by swamping out saloons, mucking barn stalls, and splitting firewood with a sledge and a wedge.

Destiny helped out as much as Bobby's employers allowed. Father and daughter shared a room and a lumpy mattress in a run-down boarding house at the rate of forty cents a day. The accommodation, Bobby said, was better than sleeping under the stars while slapping mosquitoes. But with a leaky roof and hordes of flies from a pigsty next door, Destiny thought, this room was not much better.

At first she assisted him, tackling such chores as stacking firewood and cleaning brass spittoons. She soon discovered a girl was not welcome in places where men congregated to discuss the time-honored topics of horses and women. Besides, for a girl to aide a man was unseemly, even when the man was her father.

Destiny took to wandering the well-traveled streets of Denver, and discovered a girl alone was thought to be loose. In reality, she was ignored by proper ladies, groped by single men, and trailed by staring teenaged boys, rejects from local schools.

Destiny escaped to the rented room. With no lock on the door, she dragged the bed in front of it and sat on the lumpy mattress while waiting for her pa to return. Shut in that small room with flies and a pervasive stench merely heightened her resolve to leave Denver.

Bobby disappeared for days at a time. Where he went to do what with whom, she did not know. She often feared he was injured or had met with a violent end. If so, she would have no way of knowing his fate or that anything was even amiss until someone came looking for him. Possessing no money, what would happen to her? Would she be forced to return to the Sarah Harmon Home? Such worries plagued her by day and haunted her dreams by night.

Sooner or later Bobby always returned. Sometimes he brought a pocketful of cash, other times he was broke, always intoxicated. As promised, Destiny never questioned him or complained about his periodic disappearances.

She met her uncle when Bobby put up bail to spring him from jail. Snoring and hacking while lying on the floor of the small room, Loy slept in clothes reeking of sweat and vomit. His notion of home, Destiny learned, was any place where he could pull off his box-toed boots and stretch out, where he could sleep without fear of losing his wallet and footgear to a thief.

The brothers were together a short time. Why they went their separate ways, Destiny did not know. She did not ask or even hint at a question on the subject. She knew only that her father shook her awake the night after Loy had departed. They slipped out of the rooming house and out of Denver before dawn, thus making her wish come true. She suspected the reason for a nighttime escape was unpaid rent, but did not know for certain, and certainly did not ask.

Destiny found that she preferred bare earth and a panoramic view of the night sky to that stinking, infested forty-cent room in Denver.

At daybreak Bobby produced a flask nearly half full. He tippled while leaning back against a downed cottonwood tree at the side of the southbound road. At sunup he lay spread-eagle in the bed of a hay wagon, snoring while Destiny watched prairie lands slide by. With the rhythmic *clip-clop* of hoofs sounding on the road, the farmer who had given them a ride angled south into the vast prairie.

Their first job was on the Bar-S cattle ranch. Father and daughter mucked stalls, filled troughs, and dug an outhouse pit behind the bunkhouse. Those jobs completed, Mr. Simms paid Bobby and sent them on their way.

Such was the beginning. They worked their way from one prairie farm to the next, ending up in a shack on the outskirts of a distant town— Columbia.

Chapter Eight

In the night Boy growled. He let out muted barking. Fogged by deep sleep, I sat up and looked around. Too dark to see much with or without my eyeglasses, I figured a bear or timber wolf had wandered by. I gave the dog a pat or two to calm him.

Boy barked again. He growled louder. This sound was a throaty tone, a low growl from deep recesses that meant business. I had not heard that one since we had been observed by Shiny Me near the beaver pond.

Weary from the day's hike, I craved sleep. I stroked Boy's big head to quiet him while I dozed. More noises reached us. Boy raised up. Growling again, he came up on all fours and faced the trees separating us from the wagon road. I looked over there, but saw nothing amidst the shadows and starlight. In the distance I heard the *clink* of harness chains and the crunch of rolling wheels. Out of sight, heavy wagons were traveling the road. With bullwhips popping, the commands and curses of teamsters wafted through the night.

Since coming here, I had learned some teamsters

traveled a short distance at night, pushing their teams for another two or three hours after dark. After daylight hours in yoke or harness, these bull-whackers and muleskinners gained a few more miles by traveling after nightfall. Reach poles with a lantern lashed to the end served both for illumination and a caution to on-coming wagons and coaches. The lantern light also picked up round, luminous reflections in the dark forest—the watchful eyes of deer.

Such travel was not good for man or beast, I figured, but time is money, as they say, and every step brought a man closer to pay day.

Boy snuggled into the blanket between Destiny and me, and slept again. Through it all, she never stirred. At daybreak, Boy's head came up. He growled fiercely and stood, his rear leg muscles bunched. Quivering, he was clearly eager to attack or defend.

I sat up. Destiny moaned, but she did not fully awaken.

The light was thin. Shadows moving near the tree line caught my eye. I made out a dilapidated buckboard wagon, the one with missing tailgate boards that I had spotted last evening. Drawn by two sway-backed horses, the wagon eased out of the forest into the meadow. Boy barked.

Destiny sat up, looking around in alarm. "What's wrong?"

"Somebody's coming."

"Who? Where?"

Her questions were answered when the wagon halted and three men, afoot, emerged from the dark shadows in the trees. Boy barked again.

I watched the men advance. They glanced left and right before fixing their gazes on us. Wearing wide-brimmed felt hats and long dusters buttoned to break the morning chill, two of them carried cut-down shotguns. They flanked a tall man who packed a lever-action carbine. Full-bearded, he stood well over six feet. The other two were average in height, scrawny in build. The man on the left wore an eye patch over one eye.

Barking, Boy left the campsite, intent on confronting this trio. I called to him. He halted, but his protective instincts outweighed his obedience to my voice. He did not return to me. He growled at the three men as he prepared to run them off.

"Delmar, shoot that damned dog."

The tall, full-bearded man gave the order. The man with an eye patch raised his short-barreled shotgun to hip level. Taking quick aim, he pulled the trigger. With a loud report, the shotgun belched smoke and recoiled. The blast sent Boy rolling through the grass, howling in pain. Blood blossomed from his tawny back and upper hip.

Destiny shrieked.

I stared at the wounded dog in utter disbelief. Boy tried to get his legs under him, but he fell again, yelping in pain. He dragged himself through the grass, and crawled under the low-hanging bows of a spruce tree.

I turned to face the three men, feeling unspeakable rage and paralyzing fear at once. Destiny stared at them, mouth stretched open. Something about their expressions, or perhaps lack of expression, underscored their willingness to kill without compunction. My thoughts raced while warnings from Rafe reverberated through my mind like distant echoes. Then I saw the tall man motion to the other two. As they advanced, he spoke to us.

"I seen you young 'uns on the road yesterday," he said. He gestured to the burro. "We'll take them packs. Hand over your money. Hand it over, and we'll leave you be."

Destiny shrieked again. "No!"

He eyed her. "Now, what do we got ourselves here?"

I saw a certain look in his eyes, and in that instant I knew the shriek and the scarf had given her away. The tall man spoke to the others.

"Looks like we got ourselves a girl. Some skinny girl passing for a boy."

"Go . . . go away," Destiny said. "Go away and leave us alone."

He eyed her. "Bossy little bitch, ain't you? I'll do the bossing. You'll do what I say." He paused. "Pull them trousers down."

Destiny stared at him.

"Pull 'em down," he repeated. "Pull 'em all the way down so's I can see what we got here."

"You'll have to shoot me first," she said.

He regarded her. "I can do that."

His flat stare moved to me before he looked at Destiny again. "I don't admire shooting no girl, if that's what you be. Tell you what. I'll shoot your friend here."

I saw Destiny trembling. I was scared to the bone, too. The road agent's casual, almost disinterested manner made his threats all the more menacing.

"Shoot him in the leg, I will," he said, "and, when he's down and screaming and bleeding like a stuck pig, you'll wish to hell you'd dropped your damned pants. Now, do what I tell you."

Destiny did not reply or comply. The other two men, still brandishing shotguns, looked on in grim silence.

"You gonna spare this boy a dose of misery, or ain't you?" the tall man demanded.

When Destiny still made no reply, he jacked a round into the chamber of his carbine. Swiftly raising the rifle, he leveled the barrel at me and pulled the trigger.

I went down, sprawling in the grass with my ears ringing in the aftermath of the gun's report. I was certain I had taken a bullet, but, when the men laughed uproariously, I discovered I was uninjured. Shaking, I got to my feet, aware I had peed.

I cast a sheepish glance at Destiny. Hands to her face, she cried, her shoulders quaking as she sobbed with a child's abandon.

"Missed," the tall man said in mock surprise. "Boys, how the hell did I miss at this range?"

The other two men chuckled as he worked the lever again. Jacking a fresh round into the chamber, he raised the gun to his shoulder and closed one eye as he drew deliberate aim.

"What are the odds of me missing twice?" he asked, squinting.

"Don't," Destiny said in a thin voice. "Don't."

"Don't what?" he demanded.

"Don't . . . don't shoot."

He eyed her. "You know what you gotta do."

Fingers fumbling, Destiny unbuttoned the fly of her father's altered trousers. She shook loose the shortened braces, and let the trousers fall to her feet. The three men stared as she pulled down her underwear.

"Yeah, I figured you was a she," the tall man said. "Not much hair down there. How old are you? You showing blood yet?" He cast a sidelong glance and grinned at the other two men. "Old enough to bleed, old enough to breed, I always say."

Destiny stood still, head bowed.

The tall man put his carbine down and unbuttoned his duster. Shouldering out of it, he glanced back at the two men. "A bitch never forgets her first. I'll give her something to remember. After me,

166

you boys take turns." Tossing the garment aside, he advanced while unbuttoning his trousers.

I lunged at him.

Destiny shouted: "Michael, no!"

Born of desperation, my move against the tall man was ill timed. He saw me coming. He raised his arm and backhanded me, hard. Eyeglasses flying off my face, I went down with a roaring sound in my ears and the brassy taste of blood filling my mouth. After a parting kick to my ribs, the road agent stepped past me and moved closer to Destiny.

"Lay down," he said to her. "Lay down on that blanket and spread your skinny legs. Go on, little bitch. Do it!"

I was conscious but stunned as I lay in the grass, vision blurred. I saw the tall man yank his trousers down, and felt a detached, dream-like sensation of not believing this was happening while at once knowing it was.

"Little bitch," he said, "you're gonna take me to the hilt, damned if you ain't. . . ."

The sentence went unfinished. Like cannon fire from a concealed position, a shot boomed from the trees.

The outlaw was thrown back by the impact of the bullet. Blood seeped and then surged from the hole in his chest. His arms flailed. In the next instant his knees buckled and he went down. Sprawled in the tall grass, both legs kicked until a gurgling sound came from his mouth. He lay still.

The other two men stared, frozen in fear until a second shot boomed from the forest. The bullet lifted Delmar's hat from his head and sent it sailing through the air in a high, looping arc.

Getting up on all fours, I found my eyeglasses. I put them on in time to see powder smoke drifting out of the needled boughs on the other side of the meadow.

I stood and saw Delmar and the other man back away from their fallen partner. They glanced at one another, clearly struck by the fear of a hidden gunman. Another well-placed bullet could be fired at any moment. They turned and fled. Rushing to the wagon, they tossed their cut-down shotguns into the bed. They hastily turned the team and headed into the forest the way they had come. I watched until they disappeared in the trees.

I went to Destiny. Her cheeks were shiny with tears, eyes closed. She embraced me, and we held one another. In those moments I felt a deep sense of confusion, unable to separate a mad dream of murder from grim reality. A moment later the burro brayed.

Destiny bent down. She pulled up her underpants and trousers. Buttoning the fly, she looked at me.

"I . . . I was afraid . . . afraid they'd kill you."

I could not find my voice. I managed to nod. The magnitude of what had happened here was still sinking in, robbing me of intelligible speech.

I turned to look at the remains of a man who had

just died. His body lay in the tall, green grass of a lush meadow, the bearded face in repose. Except for a blood-soaked shirtfront, he could have been asleep. The burro *hee-haw*ed again. I heard Destiny's voice.

"Michael."

I saw Destiny looking past me. In the next instant a gruff voice reached us.

"So you didn't want me follering after you, huh?"

Noah Locke crossed the meadow, shoulders dipping with each step of his ungainly stride. In his right hand he carried the old buffalo gun. In the other he held the reins of his black riding mule.

"Reckon you're singing a different song now, ain't you?" Closing the distance, Mr. Locke went on: "Hell, I could have dropped all three of 'em. Had 'em in my sights, cold. They knowed it, too, didn't they? Ever seen a pair of outlaws more a-scared than them two was?"

Mr. Locke drew up. He looked down at the corpse dispassionately. "Flapped his danged arms like he aimed to fly. You seen him. Dead on his feet with his trousers plumb down to his knees, and he's trying to take wing." He let out a burst of harsh laughter as a joke came to his mind. "He warn't no angel!"

Locke moved to the mule and shoved his Sharps into the scabbard. Stepping past me, he knelt and rifled the dead man's pockets. I watched as he pulled out makings, a stem-winder, a brass locket with a cameo, two diamond rings, and four gold nuggets the size of peas.

"Outlaw booty," he said, showing his jack-o'-lantern grin. "Mine, now."

Destiny and I watched Mr. Locke yank a boot off the dead man's foot. He swore triumphantly, and held up a wad of cash hidden in the man's sock. After a quick count, he exclaimed: "Fifty-two dollars! Fifty-two dollars he don't need no more!"

Standing, Mr. Locke placed the plunder in his possibles sack. I watched him walk in a widening circle until he came upon the carbine. Lifting the rifle out of the dew-dampened grass, he worked the lever and slanted the breech toward morning sunlight. He squinted and nodded approval.

"Kept his gun clean," Mr. Locke said. "I'll give him that."

Telling me to lend a hand, Mr. Locke moved to the corpse. I followed his example as he unceremoniously grabbed an ankle. We dragged the dead man across the meadow and into the trees.

"Bring that 'ere duster," he said to me.

With no shovel to dig a grave, we merely covered most of the body with the duster and piled rocks on top of it. While we worked, blue jays screeched and chickadees darted through the treetops, all of them merrily greeting the day.

"This oughter keep the danged wolves offen him for a spell," Mr. Locke said, stepping back as we finished. "Not that I give half a damn. Ever' critter

170

walking, crawling, or slithering on this 'ere earth has gotta eat. Ain't that so?"

I went to Destiny's side. She had watched us, her expression dulled. I figured she, too, was caught in a state of emotional limbo, a strange and fogged landscape of the mind lodged somewhere between stark reality and a vivid nightmare.

Destiny asked: "Where's Boy?"

We crossed the meadow, angling through knee-high grass to the spruce tree where I had last seen the mastiff. We found him. Boy had crawled under the sagging boughs. He lay in the shade amid dried needles. I heard him whine. His big head came up as we dropped to our knees. He watched us with those deep, dark eyes, his tail slowly wagging back and forth.

I reached into the shaded space to pet him. My fingers touched warm moisture, and came away bloody. Destiny and I exchanged a glance. Neither of us spoke, but I knew from her expression that she shared my fear Boy had crawled here to die.

Boy growled. A shadow fell over us. I looked over my shoulder. Mr. Locke made a strange, ethereal sight. Like some vaporous spirit looming out of the underworld of mythology so treasured by Mr. Porter, the old-timer's gaunt body and shaggy hair were back-lighted against the bright sky of morning.

Destiny petted Boy and spoke softly to him. I

moved closer and lifted a bough to let in some light. Blood gleamed, covering his lower back and one hip.

"Drag that 'ere dog outen 'ere."

I cast a doubtful look at Mr. Locke.

"Drag him outen 'ere," he repeated, "so's I can see how bad he's shot up."

Hesitating, I reached in and grasped one of Boy's paws. He whined when I tugged gently.

"Go on," Mr. Locke said with growing impatience. "Get it done."

I reached under the bough with my other hand. Grasping Boy by the scruff of his neck, I pulled him. He growled, but did not try to bite me when I dragged him into sunlight. Mr. Locke leaned down to inspect pin-prick wounds oozing blood.

"Birdshot," he concluded. "Ain't bad. Not yet. You gotta warsh that 'ere blood offen him. Warsh them wounds good, or pie-san will get him."

"Pie-san," I repeated.

"Pie-san raises the awfulest stink," he said. "This 'ere dog will rot to death before your eyes iffen you don't warsh them wounds proper."

I turned to Destiny. "Pie-san?"

"Poison," she translated.

Mr. Locke nodded. "What I said. Some folks call it gang-of-green. Why, I dunno. Don't matter whatcha call it. It's the stink of death. I know, for I have done smelled it. It's the awfulest stink knowed to man. Gets into your skin and stays 'ere. If you think pig shit stinks, you ain't never smelled a rotten wound. It's ten times worser. Hell, it's a hunnert times worser."

We filled canteens from the pond and flushed Boy's wounds. Most of the birdshot was just under the surface of his skin, and each one came out when we squeezed the wounds. Boy whined in agony. He yelped but did not fight us. Despite the misery, he seemed to sense that our good intentions outweighed his pain.

"I'll tend to him."

Surprised by the offer, Destiny and I watched Mr. Locke create a poultice. He pulverized and mixed ingredients with the practiced precision of a pharmacist. The poultice was composed of gunpowder from a .50-caliber shell casing, aspen leaves dampened and mashed on a flat rock to a rough paste, and green pine needles chopped finely under the blade of his Bowie knife. To this mix he added a gob of pinesap, the stickiest substance on earth. Pinesap held the whole mess together, and stuck when pressed against Boy's wounds.

We took turns holding the poultice in place while preventing Boy from clawing at it or rolling in the grass to rub it off. After an initial yelp or two, the mastiff calmed, as if the pain had left him. Perhaps it had. He rested his chin on my leg, and dozed. The cure that seemed miraculous at the time is readily explained by modern science. In nature pine needles yield oil of turpentine in a pure form. The potent medicinal qualities of turpentine in its natural state mixed with the other ingredients had the desired effect.

Mr. Locke made a new poultice every morning and evening. We camped while Boy regained his strength. The bleeding had stopped with no deathly whiffs of "pie-san." In the meantime, Mr. Locke cut willows and shaved off small branches. He weaved the flexible sticks together. Using saplings for two posts, he fashioned a lean-to. Then he cut pine boughs and heaped them on top of the woven willows.

The shelter ably served its purpose. Withstanding wind gusts, rain, and hail, the structure was remarkably sturdy. It shed water, too. We ducked for cover every afternoon when the sky darkened and thunder rumbled. Terrified, Boy invariably limped after us. The burro stood outside the shelter and braved the "thunderations" in the parlance of Mr. Locke.

Still shaken, Destiny felt fearful in the aftermath of our encounter with road agents. Nights, she clung to me, sleeping fitfully. She admitted to lingering fears. One-eyed murderers stalked her dreams. Mr. Locke overheard when she expressed her fear that the two surviving road agents would return to exact revenge. The old-timer spoke simply and to the point.

"Not while I'm traipsing around these danged parts, they won't."

Destiny's attitude toward him had changed

markedly. I noted she broke the ice by carrying food from the panniers to the lean-to. At first Mr. Locke feigned a mannered attitude by grandly refusing her offer.

"Oh, don't make no bother on my account," he said to her. "I can catch me a trout or two, and eat right handsome."

Destiny insisted, and at last Mr. Locke relented. They shared the midday meal while seated in the shade of the lean-to. I steered clear of them. With a glance over there, I saw them face one another as they spoke in quiet earnestness. Exactly what was stated, contended, and agreed upon, I did not know. I did not ask. Theirs was a private matter, none of my affair, but the mere fact that Mr. Locke had thrown in with us was proof of reconciliation of some sort. Not that peace between them came without emotional expenditure.

Mr. Locke remained stone-faced while Destiny cried with both hands pressed to her cheeks like a poultice of her own. I did not have to ponder where her thoughts ranged as she plumbed the soul of this old-timer, the man who had saved her from rape or worse, the man who may well have killed her father.

Over a crackling campfire that night Mr. Locke stated that he no longer doubted us. He took us at our word when informed again that neither Destiny nor I knew the whereabouts of the Bar-S payroll. We did not know if the money had been stolen by

Bobby Eckstrum or Loy Eckstrum—or someone else unknown to us. We did not know which brother was still alive, or if both were dead. Destiny was determined to find out. That was the reason she had left Columbia. That, and the prospect of confinement in the Sarah Harmon Home For Girls, motivated her quest.

Noah Locke acknowledged those circumstances, but at once put us on notice. He had not abandoned his search. Far from it. He reiterated his conviction that either Bobby or Loy was guilty. Given their familiarity with Revlis and the Owl Cañon district, he reckoned one of the brothers was hereabouts— somewhere.

His gaze swung left and right as he spoke. Barren, rock-strewn mountainsides were pocked with mines and prospect holes, some dating back thirty years. Abandoned, most registered claims had long since lapsed. As a result, potential hiding places for outlaws numbered in the hundreds. Thus stating his views on that subject, Mr. Locke fell silent as he gazed into the campfire where flames flared and fell back. He voiced his request in a tentative, muted tone.

"Reckon I'll ride with you . . . to Owl Cañon . . . iffen you don't mind the pleasure of my danged company."

Destiny lifted her gaze. A long moment passed between them. The burro grew restive as though comprehending every word and fully appreciating the implications—namely the continued presence of his mortal enemy, the mule.

Destiny reached out. She grasped the old-timer's gnarled hand. Boy looked on, tail wagging. The burro tossed his head and brayed as though warning of impending catastrophes. I saw Destiny smile for the first time in a long while.

So it was, then, that the three of us with the mule, the burro, and the mastiff followed the freight road into the mining district known as Owl Cañon.

Mastiff.

More than mere muscle and hide, I well remember the knit brow and those dark, searching eyes. If it is possible for a dog to adopt a human, then such a phenomenon between species explains what happened to me. From our first meeting of the eyes on the home place of the Lazy 3 Ranch, Boy had gazed at me in various expressions of trust, hunger, curiosity, loyalty, play.

Mastiff.

A word of caution. Given the thinnest opportunity, professors will regale you with their acquired knowledge, spewing more facts and figures than you ever wanted to know about a subject innocently raised. Sponge-like, professors are creatures who thirst for information. Once saturated, they feel compelled to squeeze, drizzling every drop on their victims without regard for reciprocal interest, much less the capacity to absorb it all. This accounts for those endless classroom lectures endured by sleepy-eyed students. As for that cautionary word, be warned. I am no exception.

Mastiff.

The bloodline is oft noted in Old World annals of bear baiting, bull baiting, and dog fighting to name three murderous sports largely held in contempt in our enlightened era. Hardly worthy of scorn, such cruelty is out of fashion in our time. So we wish to believe.

Mastiff.

Not named for ferocity as one might surmise, the breed is known for tameness. Proof? The linguistic source is Latin. *Mansuecere* gives us the word *manus*, or hand, and the verb *suescere* meaning "to be accustomed to." The tame beast harbors no fear of the hand that feeds and strokes it. As to the word we recognize, mastiff is first recorded in Middle English (mastif) around 1380—an old breed, indeed.

Boy.

I well remember the knit brow between deep, dark eyes—eyes gazing at me—eyes slowly blinking.

The last leg of our trek took three full days and most of a fourth. The altitude exacted a toll on all of us, and we rested often to catch our breaths. Through it all, I noted Mr. Locke grimaced while in the saddle, yet he was vigilant. He observed the wheeled traffic on the road. We did not come upon the battered wagon with a missing tailgate, that memorable vehicle pulled by a team of sway-backed plugs. We did not encounter a man with one eye covered by a patch, either.

But for bullwhackers walking beside their teams, Destiny and I were the only travelers afoot. The switch backing grades were not strenuous, but they were long. We breathed deeply of the rarified air as we trudged upslope and plodded down mountain-sides—and drank water from safe sources.

For Destiny, the rigors of the hike seemed to relieve her mind of attacks by road agents. So did the presence of Mr. Locke, I supposed, for he camped nearby. Nights, she slept soundly at my side with Boy between us. Days, a spring was in her step.

Destiny ventured a smile when she caught me looking at her. I figured I knew what was on her mind, or a penny's worth of her thoughts, anyway. Her destination, if not yet in sight, was measurably closer with every step.

The road led past an odorous trash pile heaped with stove ashes, rusted tins, shards of broken bottles, and cracked crockery. Bones and offal were scattered about as though a butcher's shop had erupted. On the far side of the dump, movement caught the sharp eye of Mr. Locke. He pointed to a pair of brown bears nosing their way through the garbage.

Boy caught sight or scent of them, too. He whined urgently as he looked in that direction, ears perked, no doubt answering the ancient call of his breed. Obeying my command, he stayed close to us. The foraging bears lifted their heads, sniffing fragrant air. Wary of the dog's scent, they turned and backed away, seeking cover in the forest shadows.

A passing bullwhacker described the location of ore crushing mills in the Owl Cañon district—downstream two miles or so from the settlement. We headed upstream, and, farther along, came to steep-roofed structures built flush against the sides of the cañon. This slant took advantage of gravity in the process of classifying gold and other minerals crushed in stamp mills and hauled away to smelters.

Thunder rumbled in a darkening sky. A fine, misting rain cooled us as we crested a ridge. The ridge overlooked the settlement loosely known as Owl Cañon. Destiny grasped my arm. She smiled at me. Boy pushed against our legs, tail wagging vigorously. Even Noah Locke found cause to showcase missing teeth.

A generous description—settlement. I had never seen a place like it. Revlis, even in ruin, had obviously been platted and designed with some measure of order for its denizens. Owl Cañon possessed no such design or even a hint of structure. With no city blocks or residential streets diagramed on a planner's grid, the place was a study in chaos. Yet

Owl Cañon was no transitory encampment, either. It was well established with all manner of miners, laborers, merchants, investors, and owners making money here for three decades. The so-called "mother lode" went undiscovered, and therefore it was a source of endless debate, a reason for prospectors to dream of untold riches.

In mining country, the search for investors was ongoing, ranging from old money to new, from all regions of America to the far corners of Europe. Few made a profit, much less a fortune. Investors agreed with the sarcasm of the era: "A gold mine is a hole in the ground owned by a confidence man." Even with all the trickery of quartz outcroppings salted with genuine ore, known gold deposits in the Owl Cañon district had staved off the boom-and-bust cycles that had spelled doom for so many mining camps.

In the settlement of Owl Cañon men roamed everywhere, or so it seemed. Gents showcased every degree of cleanliness and fashion, whether it was wheeling and dealing or picking and shoveling. Garb ranged from the dirty, patched clothing of laborers to the pressed, polished, and clean-shaven dandies who donned bowlers and tailored suits with stiff starched shirts and clean white collars. With thunder grumbling overhead in dark clouds, men swarmed through narrow passages, darting between businesses like bees stirred from a hive.

We paused to gaze upon the hodge-podge—a collection of shops, cafés, tents, squat cabins, and long boarding houses. A side street led across a narrow bridge spanning the creek to a row of saloons and gambling halls. At the end of the line, cribs were marked by lamps with red chimneys. All of these enterprises were packed into the steep-walled cañon where a creek rushed by.

To the observer, the buildings could have been randomly tossed here by a great wave or cyclonic wind. On closer examination, though, it was clear homes and stores stood on high ground, protected from the spring floods of snow melt. With few level sites, or the mechanical means to level them, structures of every conceivable shape and size had been sawn, hammered, and shoe-horned onto lots of odd dimensions.

Entering from the south, we skirted narrow streets, passages of the width one might expect in a mountain village of southern Europe. From the main thoroughfare, routes to residences were hardly more than cow paths twisting from one hovel to the next. And like the Alps, rugged mountain peaks towered over men and their works.

A few miles farther and 1,000 feet higher, one great mountain loomed over the settlement, just as Mount Blanc marked the highest peak on the French-Italian border. This mountain in Colorado embraced a glacier in a bowl-shaped cirque, a remnant of the Ice Age. Melting a few drops at a time, cold, clean water pooled in a lake as blue as the sky.

From there, the creek wended its way through a jumble of boulders to cascade over a natural spillway. Flowing through Owl Cañon, the tributaries gathered in their rush out of the mountains to countless gullies creasing the distant plain.

With scenic sights stretching before us, Destiny and I exchanged a lingering glance. Just as the rugged beauty of the region needed no description when one stood before it, spoken words between us were not required to convey meaning. I figured she was reflecting on that dark morning before dawn, thinking back to the day our trek began along the bank of Antelope Creek.

I know I was.

General Mercantile & Miner's Supplies
Chas. Coover, Prop.
Owl Cañon, Colorado

In the sprinkle of rain we made our way along the settlement's main drag. Frontier-style lettering graced the front of the largest commercial building. Two stories high, the mercantile was readily identified by its false front and an entrance covered by a wide, sun-faded awning.

Sheltered from the light rain, men lounged on the plank walk there. Either off shift or out of work, I figured, these gents chewed and spat, smoked and whittled, cussed and discussed. For their amusement and free entertainment, they observed traffic and passed the daylight hours with idle commentaries. When we drew closer, one man spoke over the hum of voices and the constant, dull roar of the creek.

"Well, look here, gents. Looky here, now, will you?"

I had walked several paces with Destiny at my side before realizing he meant us. I looked over there. A gathering of fifteen or twenty men and a scattering of women stared at us. Boy growled— not at them. Ahead, town dogs loped toward us.

Destiny cast an uneasy look at me. The burro suddenly pitched. She struggled to hold him until I grabbed the rope. Between the two of us we brought him under control with our boardwalk audience laughing at the circus-like performance.

With the dogs closing in, we halted in the street. The burro's eyes rolled in fear as he attempted to back away. Even the big mule backed up until Mr. Locke reined him in. Snarling, the mongrels bared teeth.

The mastiff lowered his head. A growl from the depths of his throat came as a warning, a baritone voice resonating with greater volume and more authority than any snarl mustered by a town dog. Even so, they outnumbered Boy. Perhaps sensing this advantage, they closed in slowly, lips curling.

In the next instant the door to the mercantile opened. A white dog charged out. Without breaking stride, he leaped off the boardwalk to the street, slid crazily in the mud, and scrambled to regain his footing. On his feet again, he made a beeline for Boy and attacked without hesitation.

In their sudden collision, Boy yelped in pain. Spinning away, he tucked tail and retreated to safety at my feet. The white dog inched forward, growling in a low tone, clearly eager to prove his dominance.

"Mister Coover!" I heard one of the boardwalk birds across the street call out. After a moment he shouted again. "Mister Coover!"

A short, hatless man stepped out of the mercantile. His gaze went to the white dog. Muddied now, the mutt maintained an aggressive stance in the street. Boy held close to me. I saw the sweeping gaze of the merchant take all of this in, and then I heard him call his dog.

"Duke!"

The dog turned and trotted back to the plank walk where his master waited. Spreading his front legs, he vigorously shook moisture and mud from his snow-white coat. Droplets of brown mud splattered Coover's trousers. The merchant hopped once and stepped back, cursing. Duke tried to follow until Coover cursed again. Halting, the dog cowered and warily eyed his master.

Coover stood under the covered entrance to his store, sizing us up while townsmen and women looked on in silence. He gestured toward the mastiff and looked at me.

"Your dog?"

"Yes, sir."

I peered through silvery rain, my eyeglasses fogged and spotted with raindrops. I wiped the lenses on my shirt. Putting the eyeglasses back on, I took a closer look at Charles Coover. He was slight of build, as they say, a dandy in a tailored suit sporting a gold watch chain and a gold eagle for a fob. His beard was neatly trimmed, pointed at the chin in the imperial style.

One did not have to be well acquainted with Charles Coover to know the style suited him. He possessed a regal bearing that commanded attention and somehow compensated for his short stature. That, and a unique mannerism of throwing his head back to peer down a blade-thin nose lent him the demeanor of aristocracy.

The town's idlers watched. Not a man among them spoke or spat. My sense was that no one dared to incur Coover's disapproval with even a hint of disrespect. At last the man himself spoke. His voice was low. The words did not carry to my ear, but I saw the men around him nod in emphatic agreement.

Then, with his hands clasped behind his back like Bligh manning the bridge of the *Bounty*, Coover stepped to the edge of the boardwalk. The mud-spattered dog was close at his heels. Coover eyed the section of street in front of his store before his gaze came to rest on me again.

"The dog's hurt?"

I nodded.

"What happened to him?"

When I did not answer immediately, Mr. Locke spoke for me. "Shotgunned by a danged road agent."

Coover's gaze shifted to Noah Locke. "Road agent," he repeated. "You were robbed?"

"Three of 'em done tried."

"Name them," Coover said, "and we shall haul them before a miner's court for prosecution."

"No need for that," Mr. Locke said.

Coover eyed him. "Meaning what?"

Mr. Locke ran a hand through his beard. "Reckon them gents larned their danged lesson in my own court-a-law."

Coover regarded him. I figured Mr. Locke would not admit to committing a crime in this mining district, particularly a killing, where he could be dragged before a jury of men unknown to him.

When I shifted my feet, the white dog growled. Boy pulled back, cowering.

Coover saw this and turned his attention back to me. "Your dog's frightened," he said. "Better get him off the street."

When I made no move to comply, Coover reiterated: "Leash him and get him off the street before he runs afoul of Duke again."

Mr. Locke spoke up. "Now, hold on 'ere. Just hold on."

"Sir?"

Mr. Locke made an exaggerated show of looking around town. "This 'ere's a public street, ain't it?"

Coover shifted his gaze to him. "Who's asking?"

"I am," Mr. Locke said.

Coover studied him. "What name do you go by, old-timer?"

"Who's asking?" Mr. Locke countered.

Eyes narrowing, Coover tipped his head back.

Mr. Locke said: "I reckon you're the one who oughter leash his dog."

Coover asked: "What makes you say that?"

"Your mutt done jumped the boy's dog," he replied, then paused before continuing. "He'll get hisself bad hurt iffen he does it again."

Coover glanced left and right, drawing knowing grins from onlookers. "Making a threat, are you, old-timer?"

"I'm a-telling you for your own danged good," he replied.

"Just what are you *a-telling* me?"

"Git that 'ere white dog offen the street," he replied, "afore he gets hisself bad hurt."

Coover mocked him for the benefit of onlookers. "Bad hurt?"

"What I said," Mr. Locke answered.

With a fight brewing, fear stabbed me like a cold blade. The white dog was a battler. Mr. Locke's tone of voice suggested confidence in the outcome of a dog fight, confidence I did not share.

Coover tugged his pointed beard while regarding us. "You're claiming the boy's dog can whip Duke?"

Mr. Locke nodded. "You got the stomach for a wager?"

Half turning, I looked up at him and shook my head.

"Wager," Coover repeated. "What kind of wager?"

"Fifty dollars," Mr. Locke said, ignoring me.

Coover grinned. "I'd be surprised if you've got fifty cents to your name."

Mr. Locke reached under his shirt and pulled out his buckskin possibles sack. He loosened the drawstring and opened it. Taking out a wad of greenbacks, he squinted as he flipped through them. "Hell, I got me danged near sixty dollars here," he said. He peered into the sack. "A couple little gold nuggets I'll throw in." He raised his gaze to Coover. "Match it. Match my wager, or get that danged puffball mutt of yourn offen this 'ere public street."

I figured Mr. Charles Coover was not a man to be pushed, particularly when surrounded by onlookers—local folks who either kowtowed to him or in some measure feared him. I think we all knew the exchange of threats and swap of insults had gone too far for either man to back down. This dispute between men could only be settled by dogs.

With townsfolk watching the drama unfold, I could keep silent no longer. I edged closer to the mule's shoulder and looked up at Mr. Locke.

"Boy's not a fighting dog."

Mr. Locke grimaced when he leaned down in the saddle to speak to me. "I'll give you the go-ahead."

I gazed into pale eyes in a wrinkled, bearded face. "What . . . what do you mean?"

"I've seen that 'ere dog answer to you," he replied. "He'll do perzactly what you tell him. When I give you the go-ahead, sic him on Mister Snowball over there, sic him hard."

I stared at him. *Mister Snowball?* This was no time for levity. With his gap-toothed grin and a taunting glance cast across the street, Mr. Locke exhibited confidence in the outcome of a fight. Echoing my concern for Boy, Destiny shook her head.

"No," she whispered. "No."

These exchanges caught Coover's attention. "What kind of swindle are you pulling, old man?"

"No swindle a-tall," Mr. Locke replied, straightening in the saddle.

"Then what's your game?"

"I aim to double my money, fair and square," he answered. "Make your bet, storekeep, and we'll see which dog walks this 'ere public street."

I saw a wave of doubtfulness cross Coover's face like a cloud shadow. His gaze swung to me, moved to Boy, and then to Mr. Locke and Destiny. From the boardwalks, townspeople watched intently. Everyone heard a final taunt from Mr. Locke.

"It ain't too late. Yank that puffball mutt of yourn

offen this 'ere public street, and we'll go on about our business."

Charles Coover tipped his head back. "Fight."

Onlookers swiftly made their wagers, most favoring Duke. I figured they had seen him fight before, and now gave him the edge over a big, lumbering dog—an injured one, at that. The other bettors gave long odds.

Mr. Locke spoke to me again. "Soon as I give you the go-ahead, sic your dog on him. Git his attention, and sic him. Hear?"

I nodded. I heard him. In truth, I had never felt such revulsion. Yet at once I was caught up in it. In that moment of heightened tension Ichabod's droning voice drifted into my mind. I recalled his colorful account of a creature from Greek mythology, Cerberus, a three-headed dog guarding the entrance to Hades.

I was aware of Destiny's frightened stare while I knelt at Boy's side. Tail wagging, he licked my face and rested a muddied front paw on my forearm. I looked into his eyes and petted his wet coat.

Here we are, I thought, *in full view of the gate to Hades.*

Destiny spoke urgently to Mr. Locke. "We . . . we have to leave."

"Too late for that," he said. "Hold the stakes."

"Stakes?" Destiny said.

Mr. Locke thrust fifty dollars in cash and two pea-sized gold nuggets out to her. "Git the money offen that 'ere storekeep, and hold it. Maybe he's bluffing, maybe he ain't. Iffen he don't place his danged bet, we'll move on."

Standing in the fine rain, Destiny seemed frozen in that moment. When Mr. Locke repeated his instruction, she turned and crossed the muddy street. I watched her angle toward the covered section of boardwalk in front of the mercantile.

Coover saw her coming. He turned, crossed the plank walk to his door, and stepped into the store. Presently he returned, halting at the edge of the boardwalk. After a moment's hesitation, he held out the money. Destiny took it and backed away. When she drew closer to me, I saw her tearing eyes. Her gaze was fixed on Boy.

"Duke!"

With that shouted command and a single hand gesture, Coover sent his dog into the street. Milling town dogs retreated, tails tucked. With his ears perked, Boy whined as his gaze moved from me to the white dog. It was clear enough. Duke awaited the command from his master to attack. He did not wait long.

"Duke, sic him!"

With the white dog swiftly advancing, Boy stood and growled.

"Now," Mr. Locke said to me.

"Get him, Boy." I stood. "Get him!"

Both dogs suddenly charged. In a blur of fur, Boy crashed into Duke. The white dog went down. Boy stood over him. Muddied and clearly out-muscled, Duke struggled to regain his footing. Boy backed away. Scrambling to his feet, Duke shook himself and attacked again. With a fierce growl, Boy raised up to his full height and met him. The two dogs collided, each one trying to bite the other.

Dodging his adversary with unexpected agility, Boy flanked him. He counterattacked and knocked his opponent down, sending him rolling in the mud while at once avoiding biting jaws. Boy rushed him. This time he sank his teeth into the dog's neck. Duke yelped in fear, and howled in pain.

Onlookers stared in shocked silence as Boy lifted the dog off the ground and yanked him downward in one powerful motion. With an audible *snap,* the dog's neck broke. He went limp. Bright red blood trickled from punctures in the white throat. Boy dropped the carcass in the middle of the street.

My mouth was dry and my voice hollow when I called him. "Boy! Here, Boy!"

Panting, the mastiff trotted back to my side. I knelt and gave him the command to sit. He sat before me, tail wagging, while I petted him. His wounds oozed blood, none inflicted by Duke.

Onlookers stared. Every man and woman on the plank walkway was struck silent by the violence of the brief and deadly battle. Coover himself looked on, speechless and seemingly unable to pull his gaze away from the mud-caked remains lying in the street.

Mr. Locke was the first to move. He touched heels to the mule and rode to Destiny's side. With Coover still looking on, she reached up and handed the money to him. She turned and crossed the street, head bowed as she joined me. Boy's tail wagged when he bumped his snout against her leg.

Mr. Locke stuffed the greenbacks and nuggets into his sack, and put it under his shirt. He turned his attention to Coover. "I never aimed for no dog to git killed. Figured Boy'd run him off, that's all."

Still speechless, Charles Coover glowered, clearly suspecting he had been deceived. Somehow. He could offer no evidence of trickery, and even though the witnesses to a fair fight were many, he seemed unwilling to admit defeat—certainly not at the hands of two children and an old man with an injured dog.

Coover looked over his shoulder and spoke to a well-dressed gent standing behind him. The man nodded curtly. Moving past Coover, he stepped off the boardwalk and made his way gingerly around the shallow puddles to the middle of the street. Eyeing the carcass, he bent down and grasped the mud-caked legs. When he straightened up, I heard a sharp intake of breath.

The gasp came from Destiny. I turned to her. She stared at the man who lifted Duke's remains out of the muddy street.

"Loy," she whispered.

Chapter Nine

The rain stopped, and tears started. Wracked by an involuntary sob, Destiny pressed both hands to her face. She composed herself, or tried to, as she stared after the man carrying away the muddied and bloodied carcass of the white dog. In that moment the sun broke through the clouds.

I was reminded of the sunny morning when I had found Destiny distraught and weeping as she sat in the tall grass on the bank of Antelope Creek. From then until now, she had nurtured a ray of hope, no matter how dim. In this instant of discovery, her worst fear was confirmed. All hope was lost. Loy alive meant Bobby was dead.

"Loy," she said again, louder.

The man turned his head in our direction, but did not halt. He rounded the corner. We lost sight of him as he carried the remains behind the mercantile. Destiny hesitated, glanced at me, and went after him.

If Coover saw this exchange, he gave no hint of it. Jaw set, he eyed me before turning to Mr. Locke. "A set-up, wasn't it?"

"I don't git your meaning, storekeep."

"This big dog," Coover said, gesturing to Boy, "is trained to tuck tail and whine before a fight. . . ."

"Now, hold on," Mr. Locke interrupted. "That was a fair fight. You seen it."

"I'm still trying to figure out what I saw," Coover said. "Your dog tucks his tail until you sic him. It's all a ploy, isn't it?"

"I dunno what you mean by that 'ere word, ploy. I can tell you one thing. If I'd a-knowed how the fight was gonna wind up, I'd have gave odds. That's for damn' sure."

Coover glowered. "If I ever find out you cheated me, old man, I'll haul you before a miner's court . . . after I personally shoot your dog."

Listening to the wrangling of men, I battled my surging emotions. I struggled to take a deep breath, and tried to think of a rebuttal to put Coover's false accusation to rest.

"Boy . . . Boy was fighting for his life," I said. "You sicced Duke on him."

Coover glowered.

"That 'ere fight was fair and square," Mr. Locke said again. "Your mutt got hisself whipsawed. That's all there is to it."

Coover tilted his head back and looked down his nose at us.

My mind raced. I thought of the remarks Gladys had made about the mastiff, the dog she had purchased from a cowhand. Then I remembered the encounter with the bullwhackers on the mountain pass. In a flash Rafe's words brought the proof to me.

"Fighting dogs are scarred up!" I blurted. "Boy doesn't have any scars! Look!"

Onlookers watched as Coover considered a challenge offered by a boy standing among men. Jaw clenched, Coover shook his head, turned, and strode into his store. He slammed the door shut. Two armed men left the covered section of boardwalk and entered the mercantile after him.

"The pot calls the kettle black" was an adage frequently cited by Mr. Porter. I recalled another: "The liar knows he cannot be trusted, and therefore trusts no one." I figured Charles Coover fit in there somewhere. Duke was a fighting dog. Boy was a pet. Coover figured he had the edge, and could not accept defeat now.

"Where'd the girl go?" Mr. Locke asked me.

I turned and pointed to a narrow passage between the mercantile and the store next door. That had been my last glimpse of her, when she had rushed off in pursuit of Loy. We headed for it.

Our little caravan followed. The burro brought up the rear, keeping his distance from Mr. Locke aboard the mule. Beyond a shed behind the building we found Destiny and Loy standing in a patch of open ground. Overgrown with weeds bent by rain, it was littered with broken barrel staves and splintered boards from packing crates.

Boy loped toward Destiny until he spotted the white, mud-splattered carcass on the ground. He wheeled and trotted back to me. I stroked his head. He held close at my heels, venturing an exploratory sniff at the dead dog.

Destiny faced Loy Eckstrum. Even from a distance the language of their bodies made a clear statement: their reunion was not a friendly one. In profile, Loy leaned toward Destiny, his hands soiled and trouser legs mud-stained where the carcass had brushed against him. With her hands on her hips and jaw jutting, Destiny did not back away from his aggressive pose.

We drew closer. Loy's curses reached our ears. Behind me, Mr. Locke reined up. He winced as he turned in his saddle, attempting to find a comfortable position.

I saw no resemblance between Loy and Bobby other than similar height and weight. Then I realized I had never seen Bobby wearing a suit—or clean-shaven with a derby covering bushy brown hair, either. That was the reason Destiny had not recognized Loy as a face in the crowd gathered in front of the mercantile, any more than he had recognized her in altered clothing and his brother's felt hat.

"Where's that 'ere payroll?"

The blunt, accusatory query from Mr. Locke surprised me. I turned to see him heft the carbine he had taken from the road agent. He worked the lever to jack a round into the chamber, and brought the cocked weapon to bear on Loy.

"What payroll?"

"Bar-S."

Loy warily eyed the rifle trained on him. "I don't know what you're jawing about."

"The hell you don't," Mr. Locke said. "Where'd you stash it?"

When Loy did not answer, Mr. Locke went on: "You're headed for the jail house in Columbia. Who's gonna get that money after we ride out?"

The implication of bribery was profanely met. When Loy sputtered and ran dry, Destiny spoke up. "I told him Pa's dead. He din't know. He was waiting for him."

Mr. Locke eyed Loy. "Your brother paid the freight for killing Simms, didn't he? Bobby would be alive today iffen he hadn't throwed in with you. That's the whole danged truth, ain't it?"

Loy had long since depleted his vocabulary, but hot anger and repetitiveness allowed for roundly cursing his accuser all over again.

Muted shouts and a brief commotion emanated from the mercantile. I caught a glimpse of men moving past a rear window. The back door swung open. Led by Coover, the two armed men came out, both of them drawing revolvers as they strode toward Mr. Locke.

Coover called out a warning: "Shoot him, and you'll hang!"

Mr. Locke lowered the carbine. He grimaced as he shifted in the saddle to face Coover. "Sheriff Hale wants him brung in. Maybe you heard. Columbia County done posted a ree-ward. Two thousand dollars."

Coover demanded: "What's the charge against Johnson?"

"Johnson," Mr. Locke said. "Who's he?"

Coover pointed to Loy.

"Hell, his right name is Eckstrum," Mr. Locke said. "Loy Eckstrum. This here's his niece. Her and that 'ere boy done hiked all the way from Columbia hunting Loy or Bobby, either one."

Coover's gaze swept past us as he considered new information. "What's Eckstrum charged with?"

"He done robbed and gunned down a rancher by the name of Roger Simms," Mr. Locke replied. "I aim to take him in. Him and the ranch payroll he done stoled."

Loy denied guilt until Coover raised a hand, silencing him. He gestured to Mr. Locke. "Where's your badge?"

"I don't need no badge to take this 'ere gent to the jail house," Mr. Locke said, adding: "I wouldn't be in this hell hole a-tall if Sheriff Hale hadn't sent me. You can take my word on that."

"Your word doesn't carry much weight around here," Coover said. "You could be lying to me now, just like you lied about your fighting dog."

"Now, don't go calling me no liar," Mr. Locke said. "I ain't gonna take that offen you, nor nobody."

Fear surged through me when Coover lifted a hand to signal the two men behind him. They spread out, handguns drawn.

Mr. Locke offered no resistance when Coover approached him and snatched the carbine from his gnarled hands. Coover glowered at Loy. "This is no place for children."

"I never told them to come here," Loy protested. "My brother, he was raising the girl, not me. She just told me Bobby's dead. He's dead, and she's a runaway. The boy . . . I don't know nothing about him."

Coover drew a deep breath worthy of Solomon and turned his attention to Destiny. "You're a girl? Wearing a man's duds?"

Destiny nodded.

"This fellow, Loy Eckstrum, is your uncle?"

"Yes," she replied.

He turned to Loy. "No matter how you cut it, that makes her your responsibility." With a glance at me, Coover went on: "I don't know where you fit in, son, but somebody's got to look out for you, too. . . ."

Destiny broke in: "Sir, we can take care of ourselves."

"This is a rough camp," Coover said.

"We can take care of ourselves," she repeated.

Coover eyed her. "Loy will look out for you. I'll see to it."

With the order issued, he turned to Locke. "If we convened a miner's court, you'd be fined and banished from Owl Cañon."

"By a bunch of damned crooks," Mr. Locke said.

Coover paused. "I'll save us all some time, and hand down my verdict."

"What the hell are you driving at?" Mr. Locke demanded.

"I hereby levy a fine of sixty dollars on you," he said. "I hereby order you to return my share of the wager . . . in the amount of sixty dollars."

Mr. Locke stared at him. "I hereby order you to go to hell."

"One hundred and twenty dollars," the merchant said. "Hand it over, and ride out peaceably. Don't look back, and don't come back."

Mr. Locke squinted. "You talk like you own this mine district."

"As far as you're concerned, I do," he said. "Now, hand over the money. Hand it over, or we'll take it from you."

"Dead set on robbing me, ain't you?"

"Call it miner's justice," Coover said.

"Call it what it is," Mr. Locke countered. "Strong-arm robbery, back 'ere where town folks cain't see what you're up to. Over a dead dog. That 'ere's the gen-u-wine truth, ain't it, storekeep? You can't get past the notion your dog lost the danged fight."

"I'm not going to tell you again," Coover said. "Hand over the money."

Mr. Locke stiffened, clearly gauging the outcome if he resisted. His shoulders sagged. In that moment he looked old—old and out-gunned. I watched as he surrendered the wad of cash from his possibles sack.

Coover took the money and stepped back. "Ride out of here."

Mr. Locke deliberately eyed Coover before reining the mule around. I watched him ride away, aware that Loy edged closer to the merchant. He jerked his thumb at Destiny and included me.

"Mister Coover, here's how I see it. These two runaways hiked this far on their own. They can just turn around and hike back to Columbia on their own, too."

Coover faced him. "Here's how I see it, Eckstrum. The girl is yours to look out for. Looks like the boy comes with her. Put them on the next coach to Denver."

"Mister Coover, you hold my IOU," Loy said. "I don't have money for coach fare."

"Well, you'll have to figure out something," Coover said. "Those two children can't stay here." He turned to his two associates. "Get a spade and dig a grave for Duke back here. Dig it deep. I don't want the town dogs digging him up."

With a last look at the mud-caked carcass, the merchant strode through the wet weeds to the rear entrance of the mercantile. His two associates went to the shed for a shovel. Loy turned to face us.

"Like Mister Coover said, Owl Cañon ain't a place for a couple of kids with no grown-ups to wipe your noses. You'd better leave directly. No telling what'll happen when you run up against the hardcases in this camp. . . ."

Hands on her hips, Destiny interrupted: "Uncle Loy, don't try to scare me. I came all this way to find out what happened to Pa. I won't go until I know. Tell me."

"Hell, you told me," Loy replied. "You said Bobby's dead. Shot out of the saddle by that old geezer leading a posse . . . ain't that what you said?" He added: "I oughta kill the old bastard myself."

"I want to know. . . ." Destiny's voice faltered. "About the robbery. And everything."

Loy lowered his voice when the two men came back with a spade and a miner's pick. "I got nothing to say to you. I ain't owning up to killing some rancher, if that's your notion."

"You and Pa left Columbia with a burro and a bottle," she reminded him. "Did you both go to the Bar-S on foot? Did you ride the burro?"

"I said I ain't gonna answer to you, and I ain't."

"I heard you and Pa talking about the Dollar Be Mine," Destiny went on.

Loy's face darkened, and he turned away from her.

Destiny pressed him. "Uncle Loy, I didn't come here to move in with you. All I want to know is what happened."

He made no reply.

"Tell me the truth," Destiny went on, "and I'll leave."

Loy Eckstrum stood before her, head bowed under the ferocity of her gaze. He cursed her.

Jaw set and her cheeks flushed, Destiny spun away. I caught a glimpse of her face. Fire lit her eyes. I had not seen such anger in her expression since our encounter at dawn on that first day of our trek. Without another word to Loy, she walked away in swift strides. I grabbed the burro's lead rope. Pulling hard to get the gray beast moving, I chased after Destiny, with Boy close at my heels.

We left the bustling settlement by way of the north-bound road. Following it for half a mile, we veered off and camped in a stand of aspen trees. From there, the cañon widened and led to working gold mines. The massive glacier was farther on, and higher up.

We saw the land-borne iceberg caught in a cirque above timberline at 11,000 feet above sea level. The glacier was surrounded by gray granite boulders and loose, black rock—the débris of ancient slides. Well below the rockslides, we made camp beside the rushing creek.

Upon close inspection, I confirmed Boy's only wounds were punctures from birdshot, not the fight with Duke. At the creek I washed him. He resisted, but I prevailed, heeding Mr. Locke's cautionary advice regarding "pie-san."

After the ice-cold bath, Boy shivered as he trotted toward Destiny. He'd had enough of me. My eyeglasses were splattered with water drops. I dried the lenses on my shirt sleeve and put them in my pocket. Then I plunged my hands into the numbing cold water and scrubbed my face.

Amid the dull roar of rushing water, I thought about ancient eras, past centuries when ice covered vast regions of the earth's surface. As Ichabod often reminded his students, the face of the earth had changed through the centuries, and our notion of permanency was little more than a flight of fancy. *A lifetime can be measured,* as he liked to say, *by a snap of the fingers, no more. In a universe too large to measure, or even comprehend, how dare we call our existences important!*

Destiny was inconsolable, her sobs audible over the noise of the rushing creek. I thought about the blow she had absorbed upon recognizing Loy today. In an instant the fact of her father's death was real, not a mere possibility to be considered later.

Now she grieved his passing, I figured, as she came to terms with hard-edged facts. In Columbia, her father would be forever cited in local lore as the outlaw, Bobby Eckstrum. Bobby, the thief, fleeing a posse on a stolen, unshod horse; Bobby, the hapless criminal, spilled out of the saddle by the impact of a bullet from a Sharps .50 in the hands of Noah Locke; Bobby, the town drunk, dead before he hit the ground. Such would be the tale making the rounds from the barroom of the Sunflower Palace to the deadfalls in Columbia and beyond, a tale told and retold, eventually logged in volumes of local history.

Boy seemed to sense her mood for he had laid down beside her and rested his coal-black snout on her thigh. He closed his eyes while she absently stroked his big head. I found them like that—a tableau—when I returned to camp. I built a fire, and, after fashioning a fishing rod from the branch of an aspen tree, I pulled four sleek trout out of water pooled from a glacier as old as time.

We ate with scarcely a word between us—fresh-caught trout and canned tomatoes from Violet. Boy rejected both, and feasted on leather-tough jerky. Afterward, Destiny stared at the flames. She leaned back on Boy, her head resting on him.

When the sun set, mosquitoes came out in force. We slapped them for a time. It was a losing battle, and we gave up. Stretching out side-by-side, we covered up with the blanket as best we could. Boy barged in, snuggling into his usual place between us. Destiny's voice reached me. I could not see her face, but heard her disembodied words under the blanket.

"I thought . . . Pa . . . might be alive," she said, as though speaking to herself. "He was shot . . . shot by Mister Locke . . . shot off a stolen horse . . . like Sheriff Hale said he was."

The sounds of cascading water in the creek were steady, much like her monotone.

"I know what folks thought of Pa. They din't know he 'wrassled the demon' every day. Pa din't want to drink liquor. He din't even like it. It made him sick. Sometimes he yelled at the demon. Pa din't want to be saddled with me, either, but he did the best he could." She paused. "Pa din't kill Mister Simms. I think Loy did it . . . but he won't talk . . . 'cause he'll hang for it." After another long pause, she said: "The truth about my pa . . . I want to carry that in my heart."

She drifted off to sleep. I lay awake for a long time with Destiny's words hammered into my mind. Only when I heard Boy's deep growl did I know night had passed. Eyes opening to daylight, I pushed the blanket aside. I sat up and put on my eyeglasses.

Boy growled again. I quieted him, aware Destiny stirred. Moments later in the chill of early morning, I heard the ringing sounds of horseshoes striking stone. Three horsemen approached our camp from the direction of the wagon road. They were blurred until I wiped the fogged lenses of my eyeglasses.

I recognized the rider in the lead—Mr. Charles Coover. He was followed by two armed men—the pair who had backed him up yesterday. Boy barked. Destiny awakened with a start.

Coover called out: "Hello, the camp! Are you children here?"

Boy barked again. Destiny sat up. I remembered Coover had hailed us from a distance yesterday, too, when he had threatened Mr. Locke with lynching if he shot Loy. Coover was a man who portrayed himself as a commanding figure, and his shouted question or command was his way of announcing his presence.

Destiny rubbed her eyes. "Mister Coover . . . how . . . how did you find us?"

"Word gets around," he replied.

"Word," she repeated.

"You two are the only children in the settlement," he explained. "Folks take notice. A laundress came into my store and said she saw you walking along the road yesterday with your burro and that big dog."

I reached out to Boy. "He won't fight again."

"I'm not here to stage a dog fight," Coover said to me. He turned to Destiny. "I'm looking for Loy Eckstrum."

"I don't know where he is," Destiny said.

"Is he camped hereabouts?" Coover asked.

Destiny shook her head.

Coover asked: "Where's the old man?"

"We haven't seen him since yesterday," she replied.

Head tipping back, Coover eyed me. "I've been wondering where you fit into this mess."

Before I could come up with an explanation, Destiny answered for me. "That's none of your business, Mister Coover."

He was not a man to accept defiance from

209

anyone. I saw him turn swiftly toward Destiny, anger flashing in his eyes. He had never come up against her, either, and, if he expected her to knuckle under, he was mistaken.

"When was the last time you had a good spanking?" he asked.

"I've never had a *good* one," she replied.

"I have a notion to hand you one," he said, the humor of her rejoinder lost on him. "Somebody needs to teach you some manners."

Boy growled.

With a hostile glance at the mastiff, Coover gestured to the two riders behind him. "My associates heard you talking about the Dollar Be Mine yesterday," he said. "Something was said about a hideout. Is that where your uncle went?"

Destiny said: "I don't know where he went."

"Don't lie to me," Coover said.

"I'm not lying," she said.

"You're all a bunch of liars," Coover said, and went on to cite proof. "When your uncle arrived in Owl Cañon by coach, he was wearing new duds and packing a fat roll of cash. I know because I held that money in my safe and doled it out to him. He proceeded to lose every dollar to games of chance in gambling halls and to women on the row. He borrowed from me, claiming he had plenty more, and he'd pay his debt in a week. He paid about half of it. To work off the rest, I took him on as one of my associates. Now he's gone, like a thief in the night." Coover eyed us. "Did that old man take him into custody to collect the bounty?"

"I don't know," Destiny said.

"Don't lie for him," Coover said. "A man like that isn't worth a lie."

I thought that was a strange comment. Destiny did not back down. "Mister Coover, I'm telling you the truth."

I found myself thinking about Gladys Quincy. She had earnestly disbelieved us, too, and simply would not alter her opinions. Coover was domineering and argumentative, and in a strange way he reminded me of her. Some grown-ups were like that. Rather than accept the word of a twelve-year-old, they merely imposed their point of view, right or wrong.

"What did he tell you about the Dollar Be Mine?" Coover asked.

I cast a glance her way. I wondered if she would repeat the drunken boasts of her pa and Loy. They had regularly high-graded silver ore when the price per ounce made thievery worthwhile to a man earning $3 a day.

For a long moment Destiny said nothing. Then she spoke softly. "I remember hearing the name of that mine . . . that's all."

"The Dollar Be has been abandoned for years," Coover said. "The main tunnel was blasted out of unstable rock. Even with extra timbering, cave-ins killed hard-rock miners . . . a dozen or more. The

Dollar Be was a good producer, but the owner closed it. Then came the Crash."

"Where is it?" Destiny asked.

He studied her. "If you have some notion of going to the Dollar Be, don't."

"Why?"

"Ask any miner," Coover replied.

"Ask them what?"

"About a female going underground," he answered as though everyone knew.

"What?" Destiny asked.

Coover replied: "Miners believe a female brings bad luck."

I saw a look of bafflement cross Destiny's face.

"Worse, the Dollar Be is owned by a woman," Coover went on with a shake of his head. "Missus Sharon Rose LaGrande of New York City bought it through a sales agent. She bought that particular mine because she liked the name. She never traveled out West to see the expensive hole in the ground for herself. Everyone knew the mine superintendent robbed her blind, and miners high-graded the purest silver ore under his nose. Missus LaGrande lost money. Then the cave-ins started." He added: "Miners say it's cursed."

"Is it?"

"All I know is," he said, "women are not allowed underground. Stay out of the mines. Stay here where I can find you. Both of you."

Destiny met his gaze. "Find us . . . why?"

"Your uncle won't help you," he said, "but I will . . . if you co-operate."

Destiny started to protest, but held her tongue when Coover advanced a pace. The threatening move elicited another growled warning from Boy.

Coover halted. "Folks will pass the hat to raise your coach fare. For now, I want you to wait here. Both of you. Understand?"

I recalled the Quincy sisters issuing their stern orders. "You can't make us stay here" had been Destiny's reply. Now in a similar situation she answered Mr. Charles Coover in silence.

We watched the men ride away. Coover mystified me. Ruthless among men, he showed concern for the well-being of two twelve-year-olds wandering through the Owl Cañon district. When I turned to Destiny, I saw the set of her jaw and a certain, unyielding gleam in her eye.

"Loy went to the Dollar Be Mine, didn't he?"

"I think so. Will you help me find it?"

When I nodded, she grasped my hand. "After I talk to Loy, I'll leave."

The remark, casual as it was, caught me off guard. "Leave . . . where . . . where are you going?"

"Lazy Three," she replied. When I stared at her, she added: "I have nowhere else to go, Michael. Nowhere safe."

Destiny stated her plan to return to the Quincy Ranch. I learned Violet had invited her, and now she hoped to persuade the other two sisters to take her in. If she succeeded, she would live on the ranch until she came of age. Then she would travel to Denver or Cheyenne to work as a dressmaker.

If you can escape the Lazy Three, I thought, but did not say aloud.

"What about you, Michael? You said you wanted to work on a farm or a ranch somewhere."

Somewhere. I shrugged as though who or when or where were inconsequential. One thing was certain: I would not be welcomed on Lazy 3 range. For me, *destination unknown* was closer to the truth of the matter. Lately I had been thinking of my father. I dreamed about him, the details lost to consciousness.

We broke camp. A passing bullwhacker pointed south in answer to our question. The main bore of the old Dollar Be Mine, he said, was located high on a ridge overlooking Revlis.

Chapter Ten

Still air in the cañon was not yet fouled by smoke from wood and coal stoves, and made a true blue sky at an early hour. In the settlement, storekeepers swept plank walks. No wagons or heavy freight outfits rumbled down the rutted street to stir fine dust. We passed through town without interference from Mr. Charles Coover, his associates, or anyone else. Even so, we did not go unnoticed.

Coover had been right about that. As the only

youngsters hereabouts, early risers took note when we passed by with our bounding dog and plodding burro. Several stopped and watched us. Town dogs ventured out on the street to challenge Boy, only to halt and turn tail when he growled at them.

From a high point, it was all downhill, as they say. With the mastiff surging ahead and the burro bringing up the rear, in the next two days we covered more ground than we had in three and a half days on our trek to the mills and the settlement. Rounding a bend on our way to Revlis, we came upon the battered buckboard wagon with a missing tailgate. Destiny pointed it out as we drew near.

The vehicle was beside the wagon road, tongue down. Sway-backed horses grazed in a fringe of grass. I saw a shadow move in the trees. Delmar stepped out of the forest with an armload of firewood. The moment he spotted us, he drew up. Boy growled in a low, throaty tone.

"Here, Boy," I said, and the mastiff came to me.

Clutching the firewood to his chest, Delmar stood as still as a buck deer. The second road agent emerged from the trees nearby. Delmar must have alerted him for the man stopped in mid-step. They stared at us, and we stared at them.

A wave of fear swept through me until I saw the two men backtrack, slowly swallowed by the forest shadows. Neither of them wanted anything to do with us, no doubt fearing the concealed presence of Mr. Locke and his Sharps .50.

Destiny cast a glance at me. I saw the barest hint of a smile on her lips, and knew the same thought had come to her. In truth, we were as eager to get away from the road agents as they were keen to avoid us. We walked past their roadside camp without a word exchanged between us.

In Revlis the stout woman we had seen hanging wet laundry on a clothesline answered our knock on her cabin door. When she learned of our destination, she offered a word of caution. The woman informed us the Dollar Be Mine was one of the oldest bores in the district, a rich silver mine dating back a quarter century to the post–Civil War era. Even before that, Spanish *conquistadores* and friars had explored the region and found silver. Taken altogether, over the course of three centuries the mountain had been poked and probed, shoveled and picked, single- and double-jacked, and blasted without ever exposing the storied mother lode.

She knew the names of hard-rock miners who had been trapped in cave-ins deep underground. Many bodies were still there, impossible to recover, her husband among them. Old-timers of the region, she said, claimed the moans of dying men could still be heard by those who dared enter the main bore.

She stepped out of her cabin. Raising a fleshy arm, she pointed to a wagon road angling up the side of the treeless ridge like a scar. That old road wending through the stumps, she said, led to the Dollar Be Mine.

Not so much a road, we found it to be a brushy, weed-grown track marked by fresh droppings and the recent imprints of shod hoofs. In a series of switchbacks, the track led to heaps of oxidized waste comprising the mine dump of the Dollar Be.

The burro snorted and pitched. I grabbed his lead rope and held on until Destiny slipped hobbles over his forelegs. Ahead, I saw the black riding mule belonging to Mr. Locke. The animal was not alone. Six mules with pack frames were tied near the mouth of the tunnel. Stacked on the ground nearby, sacks of heavy canvas caught Destiny's eye. She recognized the black sand that had spilled on the ground around them.

We left the burro in a grass-laden meadow below the mine dump. Climbing to the mouth, we passed the leavings of men—a broken shovel, a pick without a handle, animal bones, rusted tins, candle stubs, a torn flannel shirt, and weathered footgear with toes curled like the shoes of mythical tommy knockers.

I saw boot prints in the loose soil. They led to and from the tunnel. Mounted on rotting ties, a pair of rails once had been used for hand-pushed ore cars leading into the mouth some thirty or forty yards away. Boy held back as Destiny and I ventured closer.

Peering into the tunnel, I saw a tangle of broken and splintered timbers, many leaning in fantastic angles as though the earth had shifted. Perhaps it had for the doomed men in there. I ventured in far enough to hear the steady drip of water, a *plink-plink-plink* sound as regular as the ticking of a clock. We gathered up discarded candles, and lit two of them with a match from Destiny's water-proof holder.

Shadows wavered as we entered the tunnel. Tentative at first, we made our way over and around broken timbers. Behind us, Boy whined.

I looked back. The mastiff paced outside in the bright sunlight, tail slowly wagging as he watched us. For once he was not interested in leading or following. The thought crossed my mind that he heard moans. In the next moment a familiar, rasping voice came out of hollow darkness—Mr. Noah Locke.

That distinctive voice and one other drew us deeper into the tunnel. By the light of our candles held aloft, we climbed over more broken timbers and found room over or around fallen rocks. Thick as they were, the timbers had snapped like twigs—vivid testament to the force exerted by tons of fractured stone that had fallen here.

Thirty yards farther, the main bore forked. One branch was blocked by fallen rock. The other was open, curving to our right. That one led toward the voices.

The sound of water dripping grew louder. We waded in cold water to our ankles. In this stilled and chilled darkness, I felt a strange sensation, as though we had entered a bizarre tomb, an underground sarcophagus worthy of the ancient Greeks. From their own Indo-European term, in fact, comes our modern word, coffin.

Out of nowhere, then, our candles illuminated a vug. Another twenty paces, and we halted. Destiny gasped. We were dazzled by a sight neither of us had encountered before—an underground cavity lined with quartz crystals. Two or three times the size of a fruit basket laying on its side, octahedrons and heptahedrons in the vug refracted light from our candles. Some crystals were as slender as a carpenter's pencil, others thick as a miner's forearm. All of them were dazzling—dazzling and worthless to hard-rock miners in search of ore.

Destiny and I exchanged a glance. She reached out and touched a crystal as though confirming its existence. She turned and smiled at me.

With no time for admiring nature's handiwork, we blew out our candles and eased past the vug. One slow step at a time, we made our way toward the glow and those two voices.

Ahead another twenty paces, I saw the shadowy figure of a gaunt man. Mr. Locke stood with his back to us. He did not see us approach, but the man facing him did.

Loy cursed us.

I was amazed to see those two men working in concert. Clearly they had reached some sort of meeting of the minds for they lifted a heavy sack of concentrate between them. When we came upon the pair, Mr. Locke dropped his end, and Loy swore again as the sack slipped from his grasp.

"Damn it, get the hell out of the way," was the warm greeting Loy offered us.

Destiny and I stepped into the circle of light cast by a lantern suspended from a timber. More sacks of concentrate were stacked in the tunnel. Mr. Locke straightened and faced us. For once the old-timer had nothing to say to us. Loy made up for his reticence.

"What the hell are you doing here?"

Destiny cocked a hip. "That's what I came here to ask you."

"Go away, Destiny," Loy said.

She pointed to the sack. "You stole it, din't you?" When no answer was offered, she demanded: "Din't you?"

Loy glowered. "You're in the way, Destiny. Move."

"You're stealing silver from Missus Rose Sharon LaGrande of New York City," Destiny said.

At first nonplussed upon hearing that famous name, Loy countered the accusation: "This concentrate belongs to me. When I sell it, Mister Locke gets a share . . . a hell of a lot more than the two thousand dollars Columbine County hung on my neck."

"You made a deal with him?" she asked.

"I don't carry no grudge against Mister Locke. He said you and him talked. He never knew it was

Bobby on that Bar-S saddle horse. Wasn't no more than an accident that he shot him out of the saddle at that range, anyway."

"Tell me," she said. "Tell me what happened."

Loy drew a breath. "Your pa met a gent in the jail house up in Canon City, a gent claiming he had sacked silver concentrate hidden in the Dollar Be tunnel. It was a place where no one would look. He figured politicians would come to their senses someday, and the price of silver would snap back, making him rich overnight."

"Who did he steal it from?" Destiny asked.

"He died in prison without telling nobody," Loy said. "Nobody but his cellmate . . . Bobby. See what I mean, Destiny? You're mouthy as all hell, but half the time you don't know two-thirds of what you're talking about. Now, get out of the damned way."

We lit a candle and made our way out by the light of the flame. Destiny paused when we reached the vug. This time she touched the crystals as though caressing outsize diamonds. It could have been jewelry, I thought, a brooch fashioned for a giant. Readings by Ichabod and his tales of giants came to mind. From Greek mythology, the word giant comes from *gigas*. Ichabod read the gory tale of a race of giants defeated in battle by the Olympians.

Behind us, Loy Eckstrum urged us to move along, to get out of the way in a narrow passage. They lugged the heavy sack as far as they could carry it. Where broken timbers lay amid a jumble of rocks that had fallen, they laboriously climbed over the obstacles. With one pushing and the other pulling, they dragged the sack out inches at a time. They worked their way over débris, and finally carried the sack out of the tunnel into the bright daylight. Arm weary, they dropped it on the ground with the others.

Boy greeted us, tail wagging vigorously as he bumped his snout against our legs and sniffed our boots. I turned to Mr. Locke. His deeply lined face flushed, he breathed hard from the exertion. In addition to advanced age, the altitude took a toll on him. Not only was the act of carrying and pulling each sack out of the mine a strenuous task, but the next chore of loading them on the backs of mules meant more heavy lifting. The sacks would have to be loaded and off-loaded every day, too, and those long-eared beasts of burden would have to be tended morning and evening—a large task looming before them.

Loy was not a man to earn anyone's trust, but the more I thought about his account, I figured he had blurted the truth when he claimed he had been waiting for Bobby to join him in Owl Cañon. Financed by the ranch payroll, the two of them must have hatched a plan to deliver and sell the concentrate. Wealth was within their grasp. Who would have guessed? Proceeds from the sale of silver concentrate would bring a life of ease and luxury to the two brothers.

Until Destiny caught up with him, I figured Loy had believed Bobby was alive—alive and prepared to keep his end of the bargain. Then Destiny appeared. She informed him of Bobby's death. Taken altogether, that one moment of recognition when she had spotted Loy turned out to be a mighty shock to both of them.

Breathing hard now, Mr. Locke dropped to one knee. He grimaced as he half turned and thrust his other leg out and awkwardly sat on the ground. He laid back. Eyes closing, he rested there.

Loy dug into a shirt pocket and took out the makings. He hastily rolled a cigarette, and fired it. He inhaled deeply and paced, avoiding eye contact with Destiny. Then, scowling in a pose that was reminiscent of Bobby sweating out a period of sobriety, he suddenly threw his cigarette down. He ground out the ember with the blunt toe of his boot, and turned to his niece.

"Destiny," he said, "you're gonna have to hike back to Owl Cañon. You and the boy. Coover will look out for you. He knows folks. Somebody will take pity on two snot-nosed kids . . . lost in the mountains, orphaned, or some such a tale."

"I don't want pity," she said. "Or lies. We can take care of ourselves."

Jaw clenched, Loy shook his head. "You can't trail after me. Me and Mister Locke, we've got our hands full with that mule train."

"I told you," she said. "I don't want to move in

with you. Just tell me about Pa. I want to know what happened, that's all."

"So you can see me hang?" Loy asked.

With that, he turned away, and strode to the mouth of the tunnel. Calling out to Mr. Locke, he said it was time to get back to the business at hand.

I watched the old-timer come up on one knee. Grunting and grimacing, he pushed off with a hand pressing down on that knee. He straightened slowly, and stood upright on stiff legs. Teetering a bit, he steadied himself and cast a surreptitious look over his shoulder.

"Don't you worry none," Mr. Locke said to Destiny and me. "Eckstrum, he ain't gonna get away with no crime."

Destiny gazed at him, the obvious question etched in her face.

"He don't know it," Mr. Locke went on, "but after we sell that 'ere silver, I'll put him in irons and haul him to Columbia." He grinned, showing missing teeth. "When I told you I aimed to collect that 'ere ree-ward from Hale, I meant it."

Mr. Locke turned and walked in his ungainly stride as he made his way to the mouth of the mine. I wondered if he had underestimated Loy Eckstrum. They had a deal, and they needed one another to bring it off. For the moment their pact was secure. But if it was true Loy had gunned down Mr. Simms in a simple robbery, was he a man who would back-shoot Mr. Locke when it came time for divvying up the cash from the sale of stolen silver?

Destiny and I pulled off our boots and wet socks. We spread the socks out on the sun-warmed rocks. Boy had been chasing chipmunks near the mine dump, a futile and comic pursuit. Now he circled us, panting. He stopped and sat, tongue out as he seemed to smile.

While Loy Eckstrum and Mr. Locke manhandled heavy canvas sacks, we sat on the edge of the mine dump and ate preserved food from the panniers. Boy's tail wagged. He nuzzled me until I fed jerky to him from my hand. When he had his fill, he moved between us and stretched out, eyes closing.

Destiny and I ate while gazing at a panoramic view of snow-capped mountain peaks. The snow fields made a white mantle under a deep blue sky. Off the horizon, a pale day moon shone over them. Awe inspiring, the scene would have suited Albert Bierstadt, the great landscape painter of the West.

Dwarfed by the vast expanse of nature as we were, my thoughts drifted to Mr. Porter and his contention regarding the insignificance of an individual life. "No more than a snap of the fingers in the cosmos" were his words, thereby putting his youthful and cocky students in their place, once and for all.

For myself, I had a sense that we walked this earth for a greater purpose, greater even than we could name, and comprehending any of it required a lifetime of observation and meditation. At once, though, I knew when it came time to argue the point, my views would not prevail. "Mankind's high opinion of itself is a common delusion," quoth Ichabod, thereby dismissing all debate on the subject.

No matter how many times Loy emerged from the tunnel with Mr. Locke to carry out the heavy sacks of concentrate, his efforts to intimidate his niece failed. She held her ground against his curses.

I was not surprised by her tenacity. From a stony expression in a bearded face, I could see Mr. Locke wasn't surprised, either. Loy grew increasingly strident. He must have wondered if his twelve-year-old niece would tag after him forever, pursuing him to the ends of the earth with her endless questioning.

"He'll never tell me, will he, Michael?"

Destiny confided her suspicion to me, her low tone of voice revealing a dispirited mood. Surprised as I was to hear it, I understood the reason, or thought I did. With no blood relatives alive now, other than Loy, her wish was the mere assurance her father was neither a murderer nor a thief. Loy knew the truth, and, if he did not reveal it, no one was left who could.

"You promised not to chase after him," I said, "if he told the truth about your pa."

She nodded, her hopeful gaze fixed on me.

"After they load the pack mules," I went on, "maybe Loy will tell you."

The low rumbling sound was muffled—too soft, too indistinct to signal a catastrophe. A cave-in resounds with horrific noise, a mighty crash of falling boulders, the loud crack of breaking timbers—so I believed. I associated a mine cave-in with powerful explosions, with a gust of rock dust belching out of the tunnel like dry vomit from the fouled mouth of a monster.

Perhaps my expectations had been inflated by Ichabod's dramatic readings of tales from Antiquity, those murderous tragedies he read aloud with such verve. I was proven wrong when that innocuous noise reached us, that dull *thunk* and a soft scraping sound of stone on stone, that innocent sound.

Moments later Mr. Locke staggered out of the tunnel. He lurched into sunlight. I saw the side of his bearded face. It was scraped raw, and blood oozed from abrasions on his upper arm and shoulder. Waving his other arm urgently, he nearly fell head first as he gestured behind him.

"Eckstrum . . . hurt . . . bad hurt. . . ."

"Loy!" Destiny exclaimed, scrambling to her feet.

Pulling on her boots over bare feet, she ran like a deer across the mine dump to the tunnel. I saw her duck her head as she rushed in. Boy followed, but did not enter. Halting at the mouth of the tunnel, the mastiff cocked his head and looked back at me as though awaiting a command.

I pulled on my boots and sprinted after Destiny. I caught a glimpse of Mr. Locke as he collapsed to his knees. Tail wagging, Boy went to him. I heard the dog whine as I entered the tunnel.

I caught up with Destiny. She had stopped to light the stub of a miner's candle, and the light of it guided me to her. We made our way to the fork of the main bore, slowed a bit by loose rock underfoot.

We followed the open tunnel. Passing the vug, we moved swiftly past the underground formation of crystals. Climbing over fallen timbers, we came upon a large pile of rocks. The débris had not been here before.

I worked frantically to pull smaller rocks away from the pile, but merely uncovered larger, heavier ones. The stones were too big to lift or drag or roll out of the way. Fatigued, and with hands scraped raw, I leaned back in defeat.

My gaze went to Destiny. By candlelight her face shone with tears and sweat. Words were not needed. This whole section of tunnel had collapsed, closing off the passage. We both knew the cave-in prevented us from proceeding any farther, and we both knew Loy was under it, dead or dying. We could not move the larger rocks dislodged by the cave-in, any more than we could climb over the pile or around it.

I heard the brittle sound of water dripping. From deep in the mine somewhere came that relentless *plink-plink-plink-plink-plink,* an underground sound that could well have measured eternity.

"Loy!" Destiny called out in desperation. She held the candle up. "Loy!"

"Yeah."

"Alive!" Destiny grasped my arm. *"He's alive!"*

Loy's voice was remarkably close—and calm. Renewing my efforts, I reached out and managed to pry one more rock loose from the pile. Little was gained by that effort. The other rocks were too large to move. One was half the size of a wagon box. It did not budge when I attempted to shove it away from Loy. Next, I tried to rock it out of place—in vain. To my left, two other large boulders did not budge, either. The third one moved. I managed to roll it away from the pile.

"Oh. Oh, Michael."

I heard Destiny whisper my name, and saw her lower the candle as though she could not bear to look.

I reached out and took the candle from her hand. Lifting it, the flame illuminated a gruesome sight exposed by the rock I had moved out of the way. Bleeding profusely, Loy lay under the largest one. He faced away from us, pinned there, with his head above the stone shards. Even though I could see only a portion of his bloodied shoulder and partially crushed skull, the candle flame revealed white bone and torn flesh—mortal injuries. Out of desperation, I grabbed another rock, one-handed, and tried to pull it away. It did not move at all.

"Loy," she said softly.

"Damn it, Destiny . . . I told you . . . told you . . . get out . . . get out of here."

"Loy," Destiny whispered again.

"I'm all busted up . . . can't move . . . get . . . get out. . . ."

"I won't leave you here."

After a long silence, he spoke again: "Hell, Destiny, you was right. . . ."

"About what?"

"Bobby . . . he never killed nobody . . . not Mister Simms or nobody else. Bobby, he told me about the floor safe . . . he knew about it 'cause you and him had worked there . . . hell, the safe wasn't even locked."

Through her tears, Destiny stared at bright red blood seeping between the rocks.

Loy went on: "Bobby rode that Bar-S horse 'cause I told him to . . . I told him to decoy a posse of yokels while I hiked north, afoot. . . . I told him to meet me in Owl Cañon. . . ."

I managed to free one more small rock. Rolling it away did nothing to help Loy Eckstrum, but it uncovered the stitched edge of a canvas sack. I figured Mr. Locke had been tugging on it while Loy pushed. In their struggle, they must have dislodged a stone or bumped a cracked timber, inadvertently loosing a cascade of rocks from above.

"I shot him." Loy gurgled and fell silent. I thought he had died, but presently he spoke again, his voice weakening. "Damned old rancher . . . fought me . . . tough old bird . . . shot him . . . shot him 'cause he wouldn't quit fightin' . . . I told Bobby . . . told him . . . take the saddle horse outta the corral . . . ride like hell . . . circle back to Columbia. . . . I never figured on a posse running him down . . . killing him like that." After a pause, he added: "I aim to . . . make old man Locke pay . . . pay with his life for killing my brother. . . ."

Loy's voice trailed off, leaving Destiny and me with the knowledge that both men had plotted betrayal.

Over the steady *plink-plink-plink* sound of dripping water, another sound reached us, a sound as soft and ill-defined as a distant shudder. Somewhere, deeper in the mine, another large rock had fallen and skidded against others. That sound, innocuous as it seemed, was forever lodged in my memory.

"Loy," Destiny said.

Except for the water dripping into pooled water, we were surrounded by silence. Quietude settled over us like a weighty force. Beyond the range of the candle's wavering flame, the Dollar Be Mine was dark and cold.

Destiny fought off her tears. "Loy."

No answer this time.

"Loy."

We waited, hearing nothing but that sound: *plink-plink-plink*. . . .

Grasping her hand, I stood. I tried to pull Destiny to her feet, but she resisted and twisted away from me.

This was a dangerous place, and I did not want to linger. I spoke her name. She ignored me. I considered forcibly dragging her out, but thought better of it. Her last living relative had just died here, and even though the familial connection was tenuous, when she left this cold, dark place and stepped into warm, bright sunlight, she would be alone.

In truth, Destiny had been alone for a long time. But the knowledge that no blood relative was alive deepened her anguish and sharpened the pain. She had started out looking for her father. Now her father and uncle were deceased, and for the moment she could not bear to leave this dark place. That was my sense of her emotional state in those moments, anyway.

Minutes dragged by. I told her again that we should leave.

"You . . . you go ahead, Michael."

"Come with me," I said, and by candlelight saw her shake her head.

Where I failed in the art of persuasion, Noah Locke's rasping voice and pungent body odor succeeded. Stirred into action, she stood as the old-timer approached with a lighted candle clenched in his big-knuckled hand. Shadows danced as he passed the vug and made his way toward us.

Without a word of inquiry, he reached for the

lantern, pulled it free, and held it over the pile of rocks. The light illuminated blood seeping into dark shadows. Using his good arm, he slowly raised and lowered the lantern, peering into small gaps in the rockslide to examine the position of the corpse.

Brighter light emanated from the wick in the lantern. I saw the bandage Mr. Locke had fashioned for himself. The open wound to his face was uncovered. It oozed blood, but the wound was superficial. The gash to his arm had been tightly wrapped and knotted, and the bleeding had stopped. That secure bandage demonstrated a skill necessary for the survival of a frontiersman traversing the "the wild waste," as Mr. Locke liked to refer to the storied Wild West, one real, the other a mythical place existing in the imagination of storytellers and yarn spinners.

In Columbia, he sometimes drank to excess and concocted his share of tall tales. Some folks doubted his overall veracity and questioned his character, but now, as I looked at that bandage, I recalled the lean-to he had deftly fashioned and the poultice he had made for Boy. As brutal and as expansive as he was at times, Noah Locke was the genuine article, a frontiersman who embodied the dictum: "In nature, only the fittest survive." By his very presence he had proved his mettle.

"Loy's dead," Destiny whispered to Mr. Locke.

"Figured he was a goner," he replied, "when I didn't hear you cryin' no more." He paused. "You might oughter get outen this 'ere tunnel. Both of you."

At first I believed he referred to the danger of another cave-in, that rocks falling from above was imminent, and he was concerned for us. I was mistaken. Our welfare was not his concern, but his was. Momentarily silenced in his search for the words to explain himself, Mr. Locke spoke at last.

"I done told you about the ree-ward."

Destiny studied him. So did I. We looked at one another. Neither of us deciphered meaning from his terse statement.

"I done told you all along I aim to collect that 'ere ree-ward from Hale," he said. "Didn't I?"

I saw Destiny nod guardedly.

"I gotta show proof," Mr. Locke said. "You savvy that, don't you? Cain't just waltz into town claiming I done captured the wanted outlaw. Hale, he ain't a-gonna hand over no ree-ward on my say-so. Yourn, neither." Having made his point, Mr Locke went on: "Cain't bring in the body that's jammed under all that 'ere rock . . . leastwise not the whole body."

I saw him reach to his waist. Grasping the bone handle of his Bowie knife, he drew it from its sheath. He slowly ran his thumb along the sharpened edge.

Destiny stared. "What . . . what are you . . . what are you going to do?"

Noah Locke said again: "Reckon you and this 'ere boy oughter leave about now."

Destiny demanded: "What . . . what are you going to do?"

"Take the head," Mr. Locke said.

Silence, and then a gagging sound erupted deeply in her throat. "You're . . . you're going to . . . to . . . ?" Unable to say it aloud, her voice softened, her words trailing off like wisps of smoke.

"I'm taking the head," he repeated.

Destiny blurted: "You mean to cut . . . cut Loy's head off?"

"What I said. How else am I gonna claim that 'ere ree-ward?"

"But . . . but you . . . you can't!"

"The man's dead," Mr. Locke said as though reminding an errant child of the obvious fact. "Iffen I could yank his whole danged body free, I would. You wouldn't have no call to be against that, now, would you?"

I wondered if she recalled the condition of Bobby's corpse when it came in with the posse. That body was slung over the back of a burro, wrists bound to ankles by a strand of rusted wire, gruesome head wound, and all.

She shook her head.

"We cain't have us no proper burying, neither," Mr. Locke went on. "That 'ere body's gonna stay where it is under them big rocks and such. Reckon somebody oughter take the head back to the body someday."

235

Destiny turned away, hand pressed hard to her mouth.

"Now, don't you worry none," Mr. Locke continued. "I've hunted deer, elk, moose, and bear pert' near all my life. I know perzactly where to cut and where to saw." He paused. "I aim to pack the head of Loy Eckstrum in an empty ore sack. I'll tie it off and lash it behind my saddle. Nobody's gonna know, not till I get back to Columbia and git my ree-ward from Hale. Then we'll have us a proper burying. Dang, I never knowed of a man needing two graves before. Ain't that something?"

I saw Destiny shudder. In a clash of emotions, disgust outweighed revulsion. The blade of the Bowie reflected light from the lantern when Mr. Locke grasped the worn handle and rotated it a few degrees.

"Walk out of this 'ere mine. Go on now."

I pushed my eyeglasses up higher on my nose and looked at Destiny. She gazed at me in the light of a candle and lantern. If she expected me to say or do something, she was disappointed. I did not know what to say. Or do.

In a bizarre moment Mr. Locke chuckled and talked to himself.

"I pert' near blowed Bobby's head off with one shot from my old Sharps. When I bring in the head of his outlaw brother, folks are gonna say I done it proper this time. Took Loy's head clean off. That's what folks are gonna say down at the Sunflower and over to the livery."

While Destiny battled her tears, Locke muttered about his prediction of townsmen discussing his contribution to law enforcement in Columbia County.

Destiny took up her candle. I followed as she made her way past Mr. Locke. At the vug she halted and reached out, gently touching the elongated crystals. A few had broken off, probably by miners over the years, with shards scattered on the tunnel floor like outsize jewelry of clear or milky glass.

She withdrew her hand and moved toward the mouth of the tunnel. In a blinding moment when we emerged from near-darkness and stepped into bright sunlight, I heard a horse whinny. Squinting, I halted outside the mouth of the tunnel. I pushed my eyeglasses up on the bridge of my nose. Three horsemen were coming—Coover and his two associates.

Chapter Eleven

"Here, Boy. Come here, Boy."

The mastiff had charged the riders, but answered my command. He wheeled and came back to me, head up as he pranced across the mine dump. He sat at my feet and watched the riders draw rein. As usual, Charles Coover announced his arrival in a booming voice.

"Where's Loy Eckstrum?"

I did not answer and neither did Destiny. Obeying a hand gesture from Coover, the two men dismounted. They drew revolvers as they crossed the mine dump and angled toward the mouth of the tunnel.

Coover faced Destiny. "Folks saw you passing through town two days ago. I figured you left Owl Cañon to meet up with your uncle at the Dollar Be. Looks like I guessed right. Where's Eckstrum?"

Destiny did not answer. With no reason for secrecy now, I pointed to the dark mouth of the tunnel.

"He's in there?" Coover asked, incredulous. "In the Dollar Be?"

I nodded, and managed to say the word: "Cave-in."

Coover studied me. "Son, what's going on here? Is Loy Eckstrum alive?"

I shook my head.

"Dead?" Coover's eyes widened. "Loy Eckstrum's dead? Trapped in a cave-in?"

"Yes, sir."

Coover exhaled. He pointed at the string of pack mules. "Loy Eckstrum stole my mule train. Witnesses saw him and Locke stealing my outfit. I figured on hauling them before a miner's court. . . ."

Suddenly silenced, his gaze darted from Destiny to the mouth of the Dollar Be Mine tunnel. I turned and saw Mr. Locke. He came out of the tunnel, bloodied.

"What in the name of hell happened to you?" Coover demanded.

Carrying an ore sack while favoring one arm, Mr. Locke crossed the mine dump. He made a ghastly sight. One side of his bearded face oozed blood. His bandaged arm seeped blood. His sleeves were smeared with fresh blood. His hands were coated in blood.

"Like the girl says, storekeep," Mr. Locke replied. "My business ain't none of yourn."

"It damn' sure is my business," Coover countered. He jabbed his thumb toward the string of mules. "You and Loy Eckstrum stole my train. Witnesses saw you."

"Iffen you're hunting a thief," Mr. Locke said, "then you oughter be looking in the danged mirror."

Coover's gaze expressed disdain for him. He gestured to the canvas sack. "What're you highgrading this time? Gold? Silver?"

With one bushy eyebrow cocked, Mr. Locke gave the question some thought. "Two thousand dollars."

"What?"

"What I said. I'm a-carrying two thousand dollars in this 'ere ore sack."

Coover's eyes widened at the mention of a handsome sum. With another hand signal from the merchant, the two associates flanked Mr. Locke and trained their revolvers on him. Coover reached out with both hands and grabbed the canvas sack. He snatched it from Locke's grasp.

Stone-faced, the old-timer looked on as Coover untied the string. Pulling open the sack, he looked into it. Had he been struck by paralysis, he could not have been frozen any harder. He stared, unmoving. Then he uttered an anguished sound. Dropping the sack, he turned to Mr. Locke.

"You're insane," he said.

Mr. Locke met the man's gaze. He seemed to search his mind for the meaning of that word. "A fellar don't have to be loco to collect a ree-ward, storekeep. Iffen I brung in the whole danged body, dead as hell, you wouldn't say I was loco, now, would you?"

It was not a point of argument for Charles Coover. The merchant turned away. He bent over at the waist and leaned forward, placing his hands on his knees. His body quivered. With volcanic force, he vomited. When the retching ended, his boots and trousers and shirt front were splattered with spit and the watery contents of his stomach. He straightened and dragged a sleeve across his mouth.

Boy sniffed at the mess, and backed away. Destiny turned away, too. She made her way to the timbered mouth of the tunnel. Coover's two associates looked at one another. Holstering their guns, the pair ventured closer to the canvas sack on the ground, inching toward the spot where Coover had unceremoniously dropped it.

One man gingerly picked up the sack, opened it, and held it to the light as he peered in. He immediately swore. Dropping the sack as though he had laid a hand on a hot stove, he spun away. Next, in his own rendition, the second associate performed a similar dance. He looked into the sack, dropped it, and staggered away. Of all the possible contents they had expected to find in an ore sack, a human head, recently harvested, was not one of them.

"That 'ere's Loy Eckstrum," Mr. Locke said. "Two thousand dollars ree-ward for him, dead or alive."

Coover and his men drank from a pint Mr. Locke brought from his saddlebags. Then they loaded the bagged concentrate Mr. Locke and Loy had brought out from the mine. They departed without so much as a backward glance.

"Thieves," Mr. Locke muttered, conveniently overlooking his own attempt at larceny. "Gol' danged thieves."

I heard the noise. Soft and indistinct, it was the sound of old timbers groaning, the wood popping and cracking, and rock sliding against rock—a cave-in. In an instant of horror, I looked toward the mouth of the tunnel. Feeling light-headed and ill at once, I ran headlong to it. Boy stayed with me, leaping mightily until he saw where I was going. He halted several leaps away.

The lantern was on the ground where Mr. Locke

had left it. With my fingers fumbling, I dug a friction match out of my pocket, and lifted the glass panel. I lit the wick, turned it up for a brighter flame, and dashed into the mine.

"Destiny! Destiny!"

No answer came as I rushed over loose rock on the floor of the tunnel and splashed through shallow puddles. I reached the fork. Thirty paces farther, lantern light reached the sparkling crystals of the vug. This passage was obstructed where it had been open earlier today. My foot struck something—something that was not stone.

I looked down. Rocks were scattered on the tunnel floor, and lantern light illuminated skin and fabric under the heavy chunks of stone. I dropped to my knees and cleared them away. Uncovered, Destiny did not move or make a sound.

"Destiny," I whispered.

I managed to work one arm under her shoulders and the other under her knees. When I lifted her, I knew she was gone. I just knew. Light as a bird, her face was stilled and her head lolled as I carried her.

I left the lantern behind and carried her out of darkness into full daylight. Boy came loping to us when we cleared the mouth of the tunnel. I knelt and set her down on the oxidized earth. Whining, the mastiff dropped down and laid at her side.

An audible sob drew my gaze upward. I saw Mr. Locke standing over us. Like some mad prophet from a Biblical era, he wept like a child, his sagging shoulders shaking. I thought I would cry, too, but no tears came.

I covered her body. For the next several hours I did nothing but sit on the ground beside her. Boy stayed with me. A few paces away Mr. Locke lay on the bare ground, asleep. I tried to tell myself we were merely waiting for her to awaken. In time, though, the truth prevailed.

Among rusted tins and the various leavings of hard-rock miners, we found the broken shovel and a rusted pick. We used the implements to dig a grave on the mountainside near the Dollar Be Mine. Recalling the reason Coover had ordered his associates to dig a deep grave, I also thought back to covering the road agent with only a duster anchored by stones. I knew Destiny was beyond pain and anguish, but, even so, we dug this one deep.

Operating on instinct more than knowledge, I unbuttoned her altered clothing and pulled off the ranch-hand boots once worn by her father. I dressed Destiny's body in a long, white and ivory gown with full sleeves decorated with lace I found in her bag. It was an article of clothing, I figured, she had cut and sewn with the help and endless advice from the Sisters Three. I used a blanket for a shroud. Last, I tied the orange and maroon silk scarf around her neck and knotted it, approximating the style she favored.

For a long time I gazed at her face. In death, I saw

the gentle curve of Destiny's chin, her fine cheek bones, slender arms folded over her chest, eyes closed. Clothed, she looked so small when I pulled the shroud over her body.

At sundown Mr. Locke and I buried Destiny's remains on the stump-lined mountain. The gravesite offered a long view of the Revlis valley and the snow-capped mountain ranges for miles beyond.

I wished I could have stated this mountainside in Colorado was to her liking, that its might and height mirrored her wish for a final resting place. In truth, what Destiny wanted on this earth was not Elysian Fields, not a fine place to die, but a place to live. Hers was a life unfinished, her death a tragedy.

Of Destiny's meager belongings, I kept for myself the brass match holder bearing the initials of Violet Quincy. I well remember the moment Destiny had found the gift among the items Violet had given her. She had studied it with all the reverence afforded to jewelry. Her notion of beauty included crystals from a secret place inside the earth. She had died with one clenched in her hand. It was buried with her.

I did not know what else to do with the match holder, so I shoved it into the pocket of my trousers. The money, four dollars and seventy cents taken from Bobby after he was slain, went into my pocket, too. I remembered Mr. Locke's convoluted notions regarding sources of cash—opinions honed to excuse thievery, I figured. He had not seen me pocket her money. Just as well, for I may have inadvertently proved his point, muddled as it was. Everything else, all of the food and gear, was stowed in the panniers.

A bleak dawn, I followed Mr. Locke down the old mining road to Revlis. At the bottom we stopped by the creek, dropping to our knees in the shallow water. Mr. Locke used wet sand to scrub the caked blood from his hands and his beard, and washed off his buckskins in the numbing cold water. Using Destiny's sewing fabric and scissors from a pannier, I helped him rip and cut a fresh bandage for his arm. I gave him a great deal of food.

The time came when nothing was left for us but to go our separate ways. An awkward moment passed between us. Neither of us spoke. The old-timer finally muttered—"So long."—and walked away in his gimpy stride. He had never once called me by name.

I watched as he caught his mule. Grasping the saddle horn, he kicked one leg up and thrust his moccasined foot into the stirrup. He grunted and hopped, hopped and grunted, and finally swung up with one last pained grimace. He turned the black mule and rode away. The ore sack containing the head of Loy Eckstrum was tied behind Mr. Locke's saddle.

Led by the dog and followed by the burro, I hiked back to the Owl Cañon settlement, hurrying every step of the way. With no sign of road agents, I completed the hike in two days. Even Boy was winded when we reached the settlement.

I went straight to Coover's mercantile. While I would not call him an honest man after witnessing his strong-arm robbery of Mr. Locke, when it came to the welfare of a youngster, he kept his word. He issued a request for money in the saloon district and the row of cribs. His stated purpose for the charitable call for cash was to aid a lost orphan and his dog, to help the poor lad return to Denver and Columbia by coach.

I was neither lost nor orphaned, but I did not dispute claims made on my behalf. Boy and I slept on a bunk in a back room of the mercantile. The white dog had slept there, Coover said, to guard against thieves breaking in.

"Locks keep honest men out," Coover observed.

No other mention was made of Duke. I wished our dogs had never fought, that Coover had kept his mutt inside the mercantile. He should have—*one more warning unheeded,* I thought, but did not say aloud.

I figured Coover was not a man to apologize to anyone, any time, for any reason, but he did stroke Boy and obliquely admit the dog made a good pet for a boy like me. I was not sure what he meant by that. Who or what was a boy like me?

Later Coover inspected Boy from snout to tail, and surprised me with an offer to purchase him for the sum of $100.

I shook my head. "No, sir."

Coover accepted my decision without argument or rancor. He brought moldy beefsteaks out of a deep cellar where meat was stored. Boy tore into them, and ate as though starved.

In that time in Owl Cañon I well remember grief washing over me. Nights, I often wept. I terribly missed Destiny Jane Eckstrum. I missed her awake and talking, and I missed her asleep at my side. I dreamed of her at night. I thought of her minute by minute during the day. I knew she was gone forever, but at once I denied the truth. I wanted her to be alive. I willed her to live. . . .

Her death was a tragedy that brought good fortune to no one. If our lives represent the pursuit of truth, as I believe they should, then tragedy must be recognized for what it is. For Destiny, it was death on the wings of youth.

The money for coach fare was raised in a mere two days. I turned the burro loose, and presented the panniers, with contents included, to Coover. Using some of that food, he coaxed and finally bribed the driver to allow Boy to travel in the coach with me, or on top with the luggage if space was needed below.

Homeward bound, then, in eleven days from Owl Cañon, the stagecoach stopped at the junction leading to our farm outside Columbia.

With Boy bounding ahead, I carried the gunny sack while walking along familiar wheel ruts. They led to our house in a stand of cottonwood trees. A nervous chill crawled through my belly as I drew closer. I thought back to that last night here in the barn. I had pulled out nails to get venison jerky. Leaving the farm, I had made my way by starlight.

Through it all, I had found neither work nor a destination. Where to go and for whom to labor were questions yet unanswered for me. The answers would come later, I figured. For now, I was keen to face Father. That was why I had come back.

Thoughts of him occupied my mind as I angled off on a footpath to our barn. I slowed. Boy held close to me. I sensed disorder more than I saw it. Something was out of place, something indefinable was wrong or missing.

Tall weeds had gone to seed, and I figured Father had not been able to keep up with everyday chores in my absence. Then I wondered if he had been injured. A moment later I heard strange voices.

Not so strange, after all. The voices were familiar. With the barn door standing open, I saw two boys tending our plow horses in the stalls. They were thunderstruck when they spotted me.

I pushed my eyeglasses up on the bridge of my nose. Emerging from the barn shadows, the two boys walked and then came running toward me—George Johns and Joey Bachman—both grinning crazily. In that instant of recognition, that wild moment before questions were posed and answers tendered, I wondered why they were here, by whose authority they worked in our barn—and then I knew something terrible had happened.

• • •

The cause of Father's death was unknown, said to be "natural." That was the word scrawled on the death certificate Sheriff Hale handed to me.

Hale had thrown a saddle on his horse and ridden to our farm after Mr. Knowles reported Father had missed his usual Saturday buying trip. The lawman banged on the door before entering our house. He found Father in bed. No injuries, contusions, blood, poisons, disorder, alcohol, or signs of violence were found. Father simply went to bed one night— boots off, nightshirt on—and drew his last breath.

I stayed with Sheriff Hale and his wife in town while waiting for my mother. Hale was interested, to put it mildly, in the trek Destiny and I had completed, and asked myriad questions just as Mr. Locke had said he would. No crimes had been committed except for the bungled theft of silver concentrate, and, as far as this lawman was concerned, Mr. Locke would confirm that the death of Destiny Jane Eckstrum was accidental. When I stated he was carrying the head of Loy Eckstrum in an ore sack as a means of authenticating his claim for the reward, Hale was flabbergasted.

The acreage, livestock, and everything on the place was sold at auction. The proceeds later paid for my college education. When Mother and I left the Jennings place for the last time on that late summer sun-filled day, we took Boy with us. We traveled to Denver by coach, and on to Chicago by train.

Epilogue

This account of "our Chaucerian trek across the prairie to the far mountains" came to light after the death of Michael "Prof" Jennings. Prof was my father, and he lived to the age of eighty-nine. To me, he was a loving parent, an even-tempered authority figure I respected when I was young (and respect even more now that I am a parent myself.) In my childhood, I was scarcely aware of his reputation as a professor of some renown in Illinois and beyond. I knew he was affectionately called Prof by his students, a tribute more to his love for the college environment than the stiff, professorial demeanor adopted by some of his colleagues.

In my growing up years, he occasionally made reference to that "trek when I was twelve." He mentioned Destiny, but always cryptically. It is clear from this account that he would never have struck out on the journey without her. He believed myopia had in some measure shaped his personality, and his inability to see great distances clearly without the aide of eyeglasses brought out a tentativeness that made him cautious, more so than if he had been born with stronger vision.

Until I came across this hand-written manuscript stored in an old shirt box on his closet shelf, I did not appreciate the magnitude of a pivotal event in my father's life. I knew he had been born on a farm in Colorado. But I know nothing of farming myself, or life on the remote prairie, for that matter. I had only a vague impression of him as a farm boy performing all sorts of chores morning and evening, and attending a one-room school during the day. As a child in Evanston, I was more concerned with my own adventures—fishing trips, bicycling tours, overnight Boy Scout hikes—conventional jaunts, all.

I was aware my father wrote a great deal, his hand never drifting far from a sharpened pencil or a fountain pen loaded with ink. I did not know he composed poetry, and considered himself a failure at it.

The Jennings manuscript ends abruptly, and I am afraid I can fill in few blanks. The untimely death of his father troubled him, I know. I know that to be true in large part because he rarely spoke of my grandfather. He did not know in detail why my grandmother had left him, a decision associated with immense shame in those days, but suspected the rift was caused by beatings. Apparently an arrangement was made to let her go peaceably with their daughters if she left their son behind to work on the farm. Thus, two men from town came in a coach, accompanied by the sheriff on horseback.

After reading this manuscript, I can safely surmise my father was markedly changed by events he had faced with Destiny, the last cradling her limp and battered body in his arms. He was ready to stand up to his father and meet him eye-to-eye, toe-to-toe. A defining moment of confrontation with the possibility of reconciliation was denied him.

When that twelve-year-old youngster returned to Columbia by coach, he was taken in by the sheriff until his mother arrived from Chicago. She promptly sold the Jennings place at auction, and returned to Illinois with her son in tow. The Jennings family has resided here ever since.

Also, I know unopened letters were found in the farmhouse, letters from mother to son, in three years never opened, never read or answered, hidden in a mattress. My grandfather received mail, if any, at Knowles's mercantile while my father looked over the varieties of stick candy. It had never occurred to my father that some of those letters were addressed to him.

My grandfather saw fit to conceal letters, but not to destroy them. Why? Meanness? Anger? Revenge? I will never know the answer to that one. I believe it troubled my father a great deal, too, even later in life.

A number of vivid passages in this manuscript made me want to own a mastiff. Leaving Colorado for the last time, the big, gentle dog traveled with my father and grandmother by coach and train to Chicago.

Boy lived a long life in a shaded, fenced yard, my father reported, always slept with him in an upstairs bedroom, and never fought again. He surmised the previous master, a cowhand passing through Lazy 3 range, had trained Boy to fight, but soon discovered the dog did not possess the requisite meanness, and sold him to Gladys Quincy, cheap. Later, Boy called on that training, instinctively protecting my father and Destiny from attack by feral dogs and cruel humans.

As to that erstwhile frontiersman, Noah Locke, his fate was revealed to me in the form of an obit reprinted in the *Tribune* from its original source, the Denver *Post*. In this account, the old-timer had once made a "horrifying" request—that is, to redeem an outlaw's head for a reward of $2,000. The severed head was said to be in "very poor condition." With no means of confirming the identity of the dead man, the reward was never paid to Locke, or to anyone else.

Forced by later circumstances to reside at the county poor farm, Noah Locke was considered a ne'er-do-well, one who nevertheless held a unique place in local society, a position well earned as "Colorado's colorful character in Columbia."

The extent of Mr. Porter's career as the town's full-time schoolmaster and part-time philosopher was unknown to my father. In comments to me over the years he acknowledged Ichabod exerted more influence on his thinking and the formation of moral values than he had given credit to him as a youngster.

Regarding that one-room school in Columbia,

two of my father's classmates joined the Army and, with a parade and great fanfare, went off to war. Neither came back from the Philippines. George Johns and Joey Bachman died, not from combat wounds, but from dysentery, and are buried in a military cemetery about as far from the Colorado prairie as you can get.

In his last year my father said to me, in effect, that life takes on new depths of poignancy the longer one lives. The comment was not a somber one. I think he meant courage and a certain emotional enrichment are granted to those who survive life's misfortunes.

From reading this memoir numerous times, I have wondered for whom it was written. The answer is probably the same as his self-described "clumsy" and "leaden" verse. That is, he penned the stanzas for himself. For the record, though, if he left poems, none has been found. But he did not destroy this manuscript. Indeed, he left it where it would be found.

Whatever the reason, it is apparent to me that the literary gift Michael "Prof" Jennings possessed was not for poetry, but for narrative writing. This account of his trek with Destiny is a fine example of the form, if I may say so.

Ethan Jennings
Evanston, Illinois

Center Point Publishing
600 Brooks Road ● PO Box 1
Thorndike ME 04986-0001 USA

(207) 568-3717

US & Canada:
1 800 929-9108
www.centerpointlargeprint.com

m

Overholser, Stephen.

Chasing destiny

DUE DATE **MCN**   02/09   29.95
